D0758429

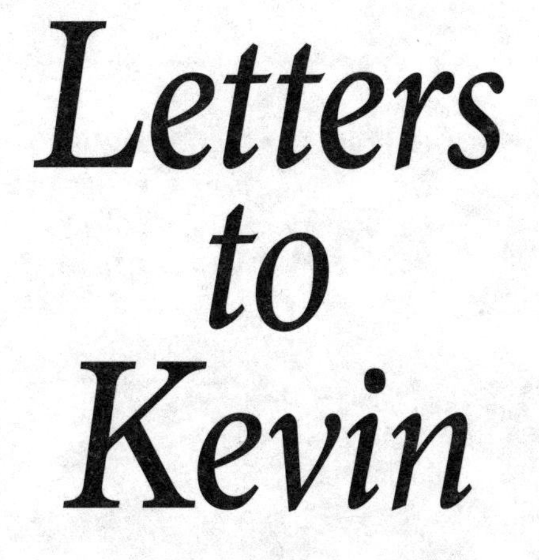
Letters
to
Kevin

Stephen Dixon

Letters to Kevin

WITH ILLUSTRATIONS BY THE AUTHOR

FANTAGRAPHICS BOOKS

Dear Kevin:

I'm writing this letter only because something keeps happening to stop me from speaking to you on the phone.

First of all, I thought of calling you from my apartment in New York City, but I don't have a phone. So I picked up my bed pillow, held it to my mouth and said "Hello, Operator? I'd like to place a call to a Kevin Wafer in Palo Alto, California."

Nobody answered, so I picked up my alarm clock and shook it to get it ticking again. Then I pulled out the alarm switch to make sure the clock would ring when the call was made to you and said to the clock's face "Operator, I'd like to place a person-to-person call to California."

I of course knew I needed a real phone to make a long distance call. But I thought using my clock or pillow would be a much cheaper way.

I remembered that the family who lives across the street from me has a phone. Both our apartments are on the fifth floor of five-story buildings, and almost every time I looked out my window to see how the weather was, someone in that family was on the phone. So I yelled across the street "Hey, can you call a number for me in California and ask Kevin Wafer there to speak extra loud into his phone so I can hear him from across the street? Then I'll speak extra loud from here so he can hear me through your phone."

A young girl on the phone at the time waved for me to shut up so she could finish her call. I yelled across the street "But my call is kind of important also, so could you please hurry up with yours?"

She put her hand over her free ear as if she couldn't hear the person she was speaking with on the phone because I was yelling too loud at her from across the street. I waited till she hung up. Then I yelled the Palo Alto number I wanted her to dial. She pulled down the window shade. Since then I haven't seen anyone on that phone whenever I look outside to see how the weather is, as nobody's let the shade up since she pulled it down.

I next tapped a message on the floor to the man who lives below me. The message went: dot dot dot, dash dash dash, dot dot dot. That's SOS in Morse code, even if the message I wanted to tap was "Could you please dial this number for me and ask for Kevin? When he gets on the phone and you tell him that you're calling for me and ask how he is, could you then tap on your ceiling in Morse code what he said? Then I'll tap back my answer to him and you can tell him in plain English again what I just tapped out, and so on." But all I kept tapping to the apartment below was SOS... SOS… SOS, as that's the only message in Morse I know. After a half hour of tapping these SOS's without getting an answer from you from this man, the police knocked on my door and asked if anything was wrong.

"No, why?"

"Because the guy in the apartment below yours has been getting SOS distress signals from you for the last half hour."

"I wasn't sending him an SOS to get help for me. Just a message to call Kevin Wafer in California."

"From now on would you mind tapping this message on your own ceiling?"

"There's nothing to tap to above my ceiling except the roof."

"Then tap your fingers nervously on a tabletop if you have to tap, but no more to the man downstairs," and they went away.

So I gave up trying to call you through the man below, who may or may not have a telephone, but who certainly doesn't know anything more in Morse code but SOS.

I then wrote a letter to my uncle in Canton, China. The letter read: "Dear Uncle. Please call Kevin Wafer for me at this number. Hold a conversation with him with the questions I've written on the other side of this page. Then write back and tell me what he said. If the other side of this page didn't come with this letter, ask Kevin anything you want and write me your questions to him and his answers. Your nephew, Rudy."

I don't know if there's any phone connection between Canton and Palo Alto. I did read in a newspaper that Shinking, a small city a few hundred miles from Canton, will only have phone service with Palo Alto and no other place in America, as Palo Alto is the sister city of Shinking. I suppose most sisters like to continue to talk to each other once they get older and move away from one another, which is fortunate for me as my uncle can fly to Shinking and call you from there. Anyway, if you do get a call from my uncle in China, ask him if he got my letter.

I then went to the street corner where there's a public phone booth, put a coin in the slot and got no dial tone or my coin back. I put another coin in, dialed Operator and got Information. I asked Information how I can get Operator. She said "Put another coin in and dial Operator."

I put a third coin in, dialed Operator and asked her to return my first two coins and then dial your number for me.

"Yes sir," she said, and several hundred dollars in coins poured out of the coin return and covered me and the phone and then filled up the entire booth. By the time I dug myself out, some people passing by had taken all the coins, the phone booth and then the entire corner. What I learned from this incident was:

1) Before you ask Operator for your coins back, make sure you lost them.

2) If you did lose your coins, make sure you lost them in the phone.
3) Before you ask Operator for the coins you're now sure you lost in the phone, shake the phone first to make sure it isn't filled to the slots with coins.
4) If the operator insists on returning your lost coins before you've shaken the phone, tell her to give you thirty seconds to get out of the booth before she pushes the button that releases the coins.
5) If she does push the button before you get away in time, dig yourself out quicker if you want to make a phone call from the same telephone all the coins just poured out of.

I went to the phone booth on the opposite corner and got the operator. She took your number, asked me to stick my change in, and a boy said hello.

"Kevin?" I said.

"Kevin who?"

"Kevin Wafer, of course."

"No, I meant my name is Kevin Who."

"Excuse me, Kevin Who. I was calling Kevin Wafer," and I clicked the receiver hook for the operator. She said she was sorry she dialed the wrong number and did I want my money back?

"No thanks. I got all the money I need from the corner booth that was once across the street on the corner that was once there too," as my pockets had accidentally gotten filled with change when the coins covered me. "Could you just dial the number I gave you?" and she said "Right away."

This time a different boy got on and said his name was Kevin Wafer.

"Hi, Kev. It's Rudy Foy in New York."

"Rudy what in the where?"

"Listen, is this really Kevin Wafer in Palo Alto?"

"Yes."

"Then you have to be the same Kevin Wafer I last saw a year ago."

"But I'm Kevin Wafer Too."

"I see the mistake now. Because I'm only calling a Kevin whose name Wafer is not his middle but his last."

"That's me. My first last name and probably my last."

"Kevin Wafer from Leary Street?"

"No. Kevin Wafer from O'Leary Street."

"Oh," I said.

"That's right, O."

"I meant Oh, like I'm disappointed."

"I thought you said your name was Foy," and he hung up.

That last call discouraged me from trying to reach you again from this booth. Maybe I'll be luckier with a booth on the next street, I thought, and I pushed the door to get out. But while I was speaking to that other Kevin Wafer, someone had parked his car in this small parking space with his back fender jammed up against the booth door, and I couldn't get out. I banged on my door. The driver got out of his car.

"Will you move your car so I can get out of this booth?" I said.

"And will you get out of that booth so I can use the phone to call my garage?"

"I can't get out because your car's parked against this door."

"And I can't move my car till my garage brings some gas so I can drive out of this space."

"Call the garage from the phone booth on the next street."

"It better have a parking space in front of it. Because this one took so long to find that I ran out of gas when I finally got in it, and I'm not about to move my car and lose this parking space till I find another spot," and he left to call the garage.

I dialed Operator and told her I was locked in a phone booth. She said she'd send a repairman over.

The repairman came in a crane. He said "I didn't bring the right tools for taking out the side of a booth. The operator said that by the sound of your voice she felt it was a big emergency job, so I brought the biggest tool we have—the crane."

"You better do something quick," I said, "or I'll kick this booth apart."

"Don't do that. Think of all the people who won't be able to call Operator to get out of this booth if you wreck it. I'll do what I can with the tool I have."

The crane lifted the booth off of its concrete foundation, drove through the streets with the booth and me in it dangling in midair, then lowered it through the phone company warehouse ceiling and set it down on its door. The repairman looked at his watch.

"Darn," he said, "I've worked an hour past my regular work shift and the company doesn't pay overtime unless you're scheduled beforehand to get it. And tomorrow I can't be here as I start my month's vacation. It would be nice to be like you and have no bosses to account to and to go and come and take vacations whenever you like," and he shut the warehouse lights and left.

Well, I wasn't going to wait a month in a booth till he came back. Maybe the phone still works, I thought. I put a coin in and dialed Operator. What I got was a man locked in a phone booth in a telephone warehouse in upper Alaska. He said "One day I also couldn't get out of my booth when an ice floe suddenly floated down the street and jammed up against my booth's door. So I dialed Operator and a crane came and lifted the booth out of the floe and set it down in this warehouse on the booth's door. Then the repairman said he had to go on a month's hunting trip, and I've been in this booth for three weeks and all I can get on my phone are other people locked in booths in other telephone warehouses around the world."

Maybe in one of my calls I'll get someone locked in a booth in a Palo Alto telephone warehouse. I'll tell him to slip a note out under the booth's door addressed to you. And that this note should ask you to call the phone company in New York to tell them there's a man with my name locked in a booth in one of their downtown warehouses, and two men without my name locked in telephone warehouse booths in upper Alaska and Palo Alto.

That's when I also decided to write you a letter to tell the phone company where I am. One way or the other, I'm going to get out of this booth. Fortunately, I always bring my portable typewriter with me when I go outside. It's the only half decent thing I own. I can't leave it in my apartment, as someone's already stolen the locks off my front door. I suppose when I get home I'll find my front door missing. And soon after that, maybe the public stairway on my floor will be stolen and next my apartment and then the building itself.

But I'm getting sleepy. I'll seal up this letter, slip it through the door and hope someone finds and mails it, and say goodnight.

Your dear friend,
Rudy

Dear Kevin:

I don't know if you got my last letter from that phone booth. Actually, it was my first and last letter to you from that booth, which now might make it sound as if I sent you two letters from that booth. But if you did get either of those letters, how come you never called the phone company to tell them where I was?

Anyway, I got out after being stuck in the booth for more than a week. The booth was hidden behind hundreds of other booths at the far end of a huge room, so if any phone workers were around, none had much chance to see or hear me. I also kept dialing Operator to help get me out. The only one I was able to reach asked for my phone number.

"That number is for a booth on 73rd and Columbus Avenue," she said. "I'll send a repairman right over."

She hung up before I could tell her my booth had once been on Columbus but was now in a warehouse downtown. I suppose a repairman went to 73rd Street and Columbus Avenue, found someone in a booth that had been installed on the same corner where my booth had been, and a crane lifted it with this caller inside and drove it to a warehouse. Maybe even to this warehouse. Because I shouted plenty of times "Hey, anybody around?" And the only response I ever got were lots of people yelling "Yeah, come get me out of this locked phone booth."

After a day in this booth, I decided to kick the glass out. But it's phone company property, I thought, which means I can get in serious trouble for kicking the glass out. But after two days in the booth I said "I don't care whose property it is or what trouble I get into, I'm getting out.

But by this time I was too weak from no food to kick the glass out. Even if I kicked it out, I'd still be too big to fit through one of the small metal window frames where the glass had been. What I'll do, I thought, is get so thin from not eating that I can squeeze through a small frame when I finally get strong enough again to kick the glass out. But how will I get strong if I don't eat? And if I do eat, I'll be too big again to fit through the small frame that I now had become strong enough to kick out.

With my last coin I dialed Operator. This time she didn't lose my coin as I didn't get Operator. I got a man by the name of Crow in Rome, Italy. Crow said he was an American tourist who got trapped in a phone booth at the Rome airport a few minutes after he stepped off the plane, and that the booth was brought to a Roman phone company warehouse.

"I've been locked in this booth for a month," Crow said. "Since I can't speak Italian, nobody who passed the booth knew what my problem was. Or maybe what I said in English sounded in Italian that I wanted to stay in this booth or that I was only making an unusually long phone call. I haven't starved because I took along on the plane a whole suitcase of American canned food, as Italian cooking in

America never agreed with me. Though I don't see why I should have thought American food in Italy would have gone down any better. But I think I'm getting out of here today. Because my booth and I are now being driven on the back of a truck to what I guess will be this booth's new place. And I can see all of Rome from inside this booth. Very pretty city. And old."

"I have a cousin in Rome," I said. "He always wears a gray hat and dark overcoat, even in winter. If you see him on any of the streets you're now passing, give him my hello."

"By gosh, look," Crow said. "There's the Tiber River and Coliseum. That's what I came to Rome to see. And here I am getting a free sightseeing trip as guest of the Rome phone company

no less. But right after I'm out of this booth I'll fly to New York to get you out of yours. Nothing less personal will do for a friend of the Crow."

He later called and said he was free and having such a great time in Rome that would I mind staying in my booth a while longer till he finished his trip?

"After all," he said, "it took me five years to save for this trip and I don't know when I'll have the time or money to return."

Next day he called several times to say how beautiful Florence was. Finally I said "I know. Lovely city, Florence. Lots of quaint old bridges and great art."

"I mean Florence Malio, a lady friend I met in Rome. Beautiful. A real knockout." Over the next two days he also said this about Venice, Naples, Pisa, Genoa and Milan. I always thought these were cities he was touring, but he said they were all names of women he'd met in Rome.

Then he arrived at the warehouse. "Sorry I'm so late," he said, picking up the phone booth and letting me out, "but I also always wanted to take a slow relaxing ocean liner at least once in my life. I tried telling you by ship-to-shore telephone, but the operator always said your line was ringing but nobody was answering the phone."

"That's because I've grown too weak to lift the receiver off the hook."

"Guess I'll have to carry you then." I'd become so light that Crow picked me up as easily as he would a fifty-pound sack of potatoes and slung me over his shoulder.

A phone company security guard spotted us as we were leaving the warehouse. He drew his gun and said kind of fiercely "Fiend or foe?"

"Neither," Crow said. "Just an American traveler back from non-cheapa Roma and a fifty-pound sack of potatoes."

"I was meaning to say, friend or dough?" smiling kind of fiercely now and holding out his hand for a bribe.

"Told you. I'm dead broke except for these potatoes."

The guard became enraged. He took a pipe and whistle out of his pocket, and put the pipe in his mouth and whistle in his ear. Then he blew. Smoke came out of the pipe but nothing out of his ear. He blew much harder. All the ashes and tobacco came out of the pipe and the whistle popped out of his ear. He put the whistle back in his ear, faced the wall and began kicking it faster and faster till I couldn't see his feet moving. But he got a whistling sound from his ear this time and the pipe fell out of his mouth.

Three guards ran into the room. They went straight to the wall the first guard was at and began kicking it so hard and fast that I also couldn't see their feet moving. One of them was chewing a cigar, another was sucking a taffy stick and the third had an apple between his teeth. But they all got whistling sounds out of the whistles in their ears once their feet got kicking fast enough, and whatever was in their mouths flew to the floor.

The noise from the four whistles was so loud and sharp that Crow forgot he was holding me and covered his ears with his hands. I fell to the floor, rolled over a few times as I thought a sack of potatoes would, and watched Crow run screaming out of the warehouse. I wanted to get up and follow him. Or crawl to the back room to try and free the other people trapped in the phone booths. But then the guards wouldn't have thought I was a sack of potatoes.

"Well, that wraps up case number three hundred two thousand and four," the first guard said, picking me up. "One of you guys care for a sack of potatoes?"

"Sure hate to see good food go to waste," another guard said. "But my family will only eat the frozen French-fried kind."

"Now if that were a fifty-pound bag of potato chips," a third guard said, "I might just take you up on your offer."

"Especially if they were onion-flavored," the fourth guard said.

"Hot-pepper-flavored is my favorite," the first guard said, dumping me in a garbage can and clamping on the lid.

That night, after the phone workers and guards had left and the building had been locked up, I shook the garbage can back and forth till it fell over and the lid came off. A janitor heard the noise and ran into the room and stared at me waving for him to help me out of the can.

"Wally gee," he said, "this is the first time I ever did see a sack of potatoes waving at me from a garbage can."

"I'm not a sack of potatoes but a man who's maybe at the end of his road if he doesn't get something to eat."

He helped me out of the can and gave me a sandwich from his lunch pail. Then he said "Wally gee, this is the first time I ever did share an egg salad sandwich on rye with a sack of potatoes. Or really any kind of sandwich on any kind of bread, though not the first time I ever picked up a sack of potatoes."

"How can I be a sack of potatoes if I talk?"

"That's another thing this is the first time of for me with a sack of potatoes. Wait till I tell my wife," and he started sweeping the floor.

"Listen," I said, "you really got me out of a jam when I needed to, so how about my helping you clean this room?"

"This will be the first time a sack of potatoes ever helped me clean a building. And surely the first time any kind of sack volunteered for the job. But sure—be my guest. Not that I can't do my job, but just so I can later say how I cleaned up a building with a sack of potatoes."

He gave me a broom and thermos of milk. As I swept and drank, he said "Do all sacks of potatoes clean up buildings as good as you?"

"I'm not a sack of potatoes."

"And a good thing for me too. Because you work so quickly and well that you'd be putting us older janitors out of business in no time. Though you did miss a pinch of dirt behind you, sack. And another one over there—the pinch you're now standing on."

Eating and drinking again made me feel healthy so fast that I swept through two rooms and continued sweeping down the hallway and up the stairs and into the back room where the abandoned phone booths were. I freed the trapped people in there by turning their booths right side up, got my typewriter and came back downstairs and said goodbye to the janitor.

"Let me take a picture of you first," he said. He clicked his camera at me a few times. "Only reason I never took a picture of a sack of potatoes before is I never found one interesting enough till now. But lookit here," when he saw the people I'd freed dragging themselves downstairs. "More sacks of potatoes. Must be a regular cold cellar upstairs I never known about. Let's get a group shot."

He lined us up in a double row and said "Will you sacks

in front please crouch down so I can also get the shorter sacks standing behind? I bet when I show these photos around my friends will say 'Why'd you ever want to take so many shots of fifty-pound sacks of potatoes for?' So maybe I better undo these pictures and take them of things my friends will appreciate more."

He wound back the film in his camera to the first picture and began snapping shots of his mop and dust pan and water bucket and the socket string of the ceiling light bulb.

Most of the people I freed crawled out of the building and around the corner. A few crawled into the phone booths in front of the telephone building and immediately got trapped inside. I felt that until phone service improved in this country, I'd be unable to call you without running into one difficulty after another. The only way I'd be sure of speaking to you again in the near future is to travel to Palo Alto and see you face to face.

I'll start out to see you as soon as I finish this letter and drop it in a mailbox. The way my luck's been changing for the better lately, I might even reach you before the letter does. If I do, then maybe I should stick the letter in my pocket so it can at least reach you at the same time.

Truth is, I think this letter has a much better chance of reaching you first. I could try and help myself get there before it by addressing the envelope wrong and not putting on a stamp. But that might ruin the letter's chance of ever reaching you, and then you wouldn't know I was on my way to see you. What I could do is give myself a head start on the letter by waiting till I got halfway across the country before I dropped it in a mailbox. And to get an even bigger lead on the letter, I could double back to New York once I got halfway across the country, and then drop the letter in a mailbox.

But maybe after getting halfway across the country and doubling back to New York with me, the letter will get discouraged that it will ever reach you or maybe keel over from traveler's fatigue and drop out of this race against me. Or I might get tired and be the one to drop out, which will mean I won't get to California. And if I don't get there and this letter also drops out of the race, you'll never know we were in a race to get to you unless I send another letter telling you about it. I can even send this same letter inside the envelope of another letter, if it's still too tired or discouraged to make it across the country on its own. But to give this first letter and me an even chance to get to you, I better just stick it in a mailbox and start out to see you myself right away.

If this letter does reach you before I do, give it a prize of something like a whole row of uncanceled stamps across its envelope, but don't let its win go to its head. You can tell it from me that I didn't have the entire U.S. Postal Service helping me to get across the country as it did, or even one mailman to carry me a step closer to your door. But the race is on, this letter is going into the mailbox, I'm on my way to see you, also, and may the better competitor win.

Yours sincerely,
Rudy

TAXI

Dear Kevin:

If my last letter ever gets out of its mailbox and is sent to you in even three times the normal number of mailing days, I'm sure it will reach you long before me. Because even if it hasn't been three times the normal number of mailing days since I started out to see you, by the way I'm going it will take me as long as it would a letter traveling to you from New York by ship with several stops to sightsee. Let me explain.

First thing, I got in a cab in front of the phone building and said "Kennedy Airport, please." I was going to take the first plane leaving for San Francisco and then bus the fifteen miles to you from the San Francisco Airport.

The cabby drove to the airport, pulled up in front of an airline terminal and said "Twenty dollars."

"Twenty dollars?" I said. I thought that was a lot of money for a cab ride, but all right. I was in a rush to see you and win that race against the letter, and he did drive well. It was also an especially lot of money for me as I didn't have a cent.

"Just a second while I find my money," I said. I reached behind me, fingered around between the seat's padding for loose change that other passengers might have lost, and found a quarter.

"Here's a twenty-five-cent tip for you, my good man, and thanks very much."

"You're very much welcome. Now what about my twenty-dollar fare?"

"Listen. I heard you drivers like to squeeze as much money as possible out of your passengers, but this is going too far. I was nice enough to give you a tip when not every rider does, right?"

"Right," he said. "But only for this time, what do you say I give you back your quarter tip for my twenty-dollar fare?"

"You've no reason to tip me. It would be different if we had exchanged seats from the beginning and I had driven you out here and talked your ears off and you had sat back and enjoyed the scenery and smooth ride. No, it wouldn't be fair."

"And what would be fair—your not giving me my fare?"

This time he was right. So I got back in his cab and he drove to the city. Now we were even. He gave me back my tip, I didn't give him his fare, and we were just where we started from: him cruising the street for passengers and me looking for a cab in front of the phone building.

I hailed another cab and said "Drive me in the direction of Kennedy Airport as far as a quarter will take me."

The cabby said "The lowest starting fare is two dollars. Then it's twenty cents for each additional sixth of a mile after that."

"Then drive to the airport in reverse. That way, when the meter goes down from two dollars to twenty-five cents, you can raise the meter flag no matter where we are and I'll get out and pay you a quarter."

I closed my eyes and relaxed as the cab drove in reverse. At least I was on my way again, or again way my on. The meter dropped from two dollars to a dollar-eighty to one-sixty and so on till it reached twenty cents. The driver stopped the cab, raised the meter flag and said "This is where you agreed to be let off."

"But the meter doesn't say twenty-five cents."

"It says twenty cents. Taxi meters only go up and back a notch by dimes, not nickels."

"Then I'd like my five cents change."

"Fair enough," she said.

"Now that you mention it, the fare's too much, I'd like it to be nothing all the way to the airport. But I guess you can't expect everything."

"You mean you can't expect nothing."

"I feel I should at least get something for nothing."

"Something for nothing I can give you," and she got out of the cab and pushed it six more inches in reverse.

I gave her the quarter and she handed me my change. I wanted to give her the nickel as a tip, but that would have left me penniless. Or at least nickel-less, since I was sure I could turn up a penny if I searched through all my pockets.

I got out of the cab. What she'd done was drive in reverse around the block and leave me in front of the phone building. And I now had twenty cents less than when I started out with her and only a nickel to my name. But I'd change that. I searched through all my pockets, but couldn't turn up the penny I was so convinced I could. So even though I still had a nickel, I was now penniless.

Only thing to do next was hail another cab to the airport, as no planes took off from the streets around the phone building or any streets in the city that I knew of. Though say a plane did take off from one of these streets and I got on it, that plane might be flying to Lisbon or London or places like that while I wanted to get to San Francisco—the closest city to Palo Alto with a major airport.

I hailed another cab. "Where you want to go?" the driver said.

"Eventually, I'd like to get to Palo Alto, California."

"Let me check the taxi rates." He opened a book for out-of-town hauls and said "The fare from New York to Palo Alto is three and a half cents."

"Fine," I said, "as I've still got a nickel."

"Can't take you then, as I have no change," and he drove off.

I walked a few blocks, thinking I'd have better luck getting a cab somewhere else, and saw a bus stop. I waited till a bus came, and just as the sign said, the bus stopped.

I got on and said "Does this bus go to Palo Alto, California, perhaps?"

"No," the driver said, "the next one does." He laughed into his hand. A few passengers sitting behind him snickered into their hands too.

"Where does this bus go to then?"

"Menlo Park, California. That's the next town over from Palo Alto, which will be okay for you if you don't mind the short walk."

"I can always hitch from Menlo if the short walk's too far."

"Never thought of that," and he laughed again. But this time he broke up and all the passengers doubled over in their seats and broke up with laughs too. I looked around, wondering what was causing it.

Then I saw. My typewriter case was open and my typewriter could be seen, I quickly snapped it shut.

"I'm glad you did that," the driver said. "It was too embarrassing to tell you about it and I thought it best not to say anything till you found out yourself. Now that you know about it, I guess I can talk about your case being open. Though now that your case is closed, I suppose it's wrong speaking about it being open unless it becomes open again."

"If there's any problem, I'll gladly open it again if you want."

"No. It would be too embarrassing to tell you that it's open if you did. And then everyone in the bus and I would start busting a gut over it being open again and you wouldn't know what we were laughing at. And I'd want to tell you that it's because your case is open, but I'd be too embarrassed to say it to your face."

"I could turn around and you could say it to my back."

"No. Bus regulations are very explicit that passengers, unless moving to the rear please, must face front at all times."

He closed the door and drove off, even though there wasn't a sign at the corner that said "BUS GO." But that was his business.

If the police caught him going through a bus stop sign, he'd be the one breaking the law, not us. As for me, whenever I walk I try to avoid streets that have stop signs at their corners. Because if there isn't another sign that says "GO," I usually stand there a long time waiting for some street workers to erect a "GO" sign or at least take away the stop sign or lay it on its side, upside down, so I can't see it.

I sat in the one seat that wasn't taken.

"Didn't you forget something, buddy?" the driver said.

I looked at the men and boys in the bus to see if anyone by the name of Buddy was going to answer him. They were all staring at me as if they thought my name was Buddy, so I said to the driver "Did you mean me?"

"I didn't mean my Aunt Tilly."

"That's a coincidence," I said. "Because I also have an Aunt Tilly and it isn't a common name."

"You do? Well, how is your Aunt Tilly these days?"

"Fine, thanks. How's your Aunt Tilly?"

"She's fine also. And how is your Aunt Tilly?" he asked the boy seated right behind him.

"Great, I guess. How's your Aunt Tilly?" the boy asked the woman beside him.

"Never better," she said, "and it's so sweet of you to ask. But how is your Aunt Tilly?" she said to the man across the aisle from her.

"Doing wonderful," he said. "Pulse is strong, temperature's back to normal. But how is your Aunt Tilly?" he asked the woman next to him.

"I am Aunt Tilly," she said.

"Aunt Tilly," he said. "I haven't seen you for so long, I didn't recognize you."

"I was patiently sitting here waiting for you to say something, but you were never a thoughtful nephew."

"Well, you have changed."

"She's gotten heavier," the driver said.

"I'd say lighter," the man said.

"I'm the same weight I was thirty years ago," she said. "Maybe a little heavier here and lighter there, but pound for pound, the same."

"I've never seen my Aunt Tilly till now," the boy said, "so I can't say what she looked like before."

"By the way," the driver said, after he stopped at several bus stops and then drove past them and broke the same law several more times. "Didn't you forget something?"

"You still mean me?" I said.

"You can be sure I'm not talking about our Aunt Tilly again."

"She's looking very well," I said.

"I still think she's gotten heavier."

"Lighter," the man sitting beside her said.

"I do wish you people would stop throwing my weight around," Aunt Tilly said.

"And I'm still saying you forgot something when you got on," the driver said to me.

I felt my clothes and looked in my typewriter case. Everything I had on me when I stepped into the bus was still here that I could tell.

"Why didn't you let me know when I got on that I forgot something?" I said. "Now I'll have to walk back to the stop you picked me up at if what I forgot there is important."

"You won't have to walk back anywhere if you never had a wallet on you or sufficient fare." He stopped the bus and opened the door. "Out."

"If I find the wallet I never had, can I stay on?"

"If you can fit that wallet through the coin box slots and it's got the right fare in it, you got a deal."

I stepped out. Everyone waved goodbye to me. Aunt Tilly slid open her window and said as the bus pulled away "Hope to see you in California, nephew dear. And give my love to my brother." It was the first bus I rode on where the driver and all the passengers were related.

The next bus that stopped had no passengers.

"The driver of the last bus said that this one goes to Palo Alto," I said.

"Somebody's been pulling your leg," the driver said. "Yeah, I can see from here—one leg's much longer than the other. That must have been the one that was pulled."

"My right leg seems longer than the left because it's standing on the top step while the left leg is on the bottom. But when I stand straight they're the same size."

"You're right. Now I can see. Though you're still wrong, as this bus doesn't go to Palo Alto, but went, I just came back and am returning to the bus barn."

"Is the barn in the direction of Kennedy Airport?"

"It is," but he pointed to the route sign above the front window which said NO PASSENGERS. I should have quickly written and held up a sign which said THAT'S RIGHT: YOU HAVE HO PASSENGERS. Or another that read WHY DON'T YOU CHANGE YOUR ROUTE SIGN TO ONE WHICH SAYS "PASSENGERS NOW ALLOWED ALL THE WAY FREE TO PALO ALTO, FOOD AND BEVERAGES INCLUDED"?

Another bus stopped. Its route sign said TO AIRPORT. NEXT BUS TO PALO ALTO IN TWO YEARS.

I got on this bus and dropped my nickel in the coin box.

"The fare to the airport is a dollar-seventy," the driver said.

"How'd you know I was even going to the airport?"

"I can read your mind." He pointed to the door for me to leave.

"If you can read my mind so well, what's on it now?"

"First, you're thinking you just dropped your last nickel in my coin box when you knew all along the fare had to be more. Second, you're now going to try and con back that nickel somehow. And third, that you know you'll ultimately have to leave this bus without that nickel, as drivers can't return any money once it's inside the coin box."

"I don't insist on getting that exact same nickel back. You can give me one from your pocket."

"I don't have a nickel in my pocket, only a dime."

"Then give me a dime and I'll give you a nickel change."

"If you can give me a nickel change when you have no money on you, I'll eat your hat."

"I don't have a hat. I do have a jacket though. It's a bit old and dirty and so probably not as tasty and fresh as my new hat at home is. But if my jacket won't do, I can always take off one of my socks or shoes."

"Just your jacket, if you can make change when you haven't a single cent on you."

All this talk was going on while the bus was speeding to the airport. So no matter who won the bet, I was at least getting closer to Palo Alto all the time.

"Okay," the driver said, "here's my dime. Now let me see your change."

"I'm sorry, but I never change in front of anyone I just met. And certainly not in front of all these strangers," and I pointed to the passengers. "I could be arrested. Besides, I'm quite shy."

"You mean you're quite broke." He snatched back his dime, stopped the bus, opened the door and kicked me out.

So here I was: in nowhere. That's what the city limits sign said: WELCOME TO NOWHERE, NEW YORK. I'd never heard of the place or seen it on a map. It was a very gloomy-looking town also. All the lights in the buildings and stores were off. In fact, there weren't any buildings or stores. There were streetlights though, but no streets. The entire town was one big sidewalk everywhere I looked.

"You drove on the sidewalk," I screamed at the bus, which was now only a moving dot in the distance. Or maybe what I was yelling at was a moving dot very close to my eyes, and the bus had long gone out of sight. "Driving on the sidewalk is against the law," I continued to yell. "People can be run over that way. They can also get hurt."

Actually there weren't any people around either. It was the most deserted town I'd ever seen. Nothing but sidewalks, lampposts and sign after sign on top of sign which said SETTLE

IN NOWHERE... NOWHERE IS THE COMING PLACE TO BE... RAISE YOUR CHILDREN IN NOWHERE... SPEND YOUR GOLDEN YEARS IN NOWHERE... YOUR DOLLARS WORK IN NOWHERE... THE BEST SCHOOLS AND CITY SERVICES ARE IN NOWHERE... FIND HEALTH, HAPPINESS AND FRIENDLY NEIGHBORS IN NOWHERE. And smaller signs on the lampposts which said NOWHERE STREET and NOWHERE LANE and NOWHERE BOULEVARD and KEEP NOWHERE BEAUTIFUL and FOR A BETTER NOWHERE: OBEY ITS LAWS AND POLICE.

By this time I was getting hungry and of course there were no food shops. I also had to make a move fast if I was going to beat that last letter to Palo Alto. That might sound childish to you, but a man has his pride. When I enter a race, it's to win, not to come second-best to a letter which wasn't even sent special delivery or air mail.

I walked in the direction the bus had gone, thinking I'd eventually get to the airport that way. After a few miles of seeing nothing but sidewalk, I sat down and began writing this letter. I'll leave the letter on the sidewalk when I get up to walk again. My idea is that maybe the next bus will see the letter and stop to pick it up, even if I don't leave it at a bus stop.

This letter I won't race though. I don't see how I can race two letters in two different places at one time. And maybe the bus that picks up this letter will see me later on and stop for me too. If that happens, I might end up sitting on the seat next to my letter. Or if the bus is crowded, then standing beside my letter while it sits in its seat. Then I'll ask the driver if I could mail my letter. I don't see why he should mind. After all, I don't know of any laws that stop a man from mailing his own letter, unless he's in prison and he's only allowed to mail three letters a month, as some prisons do. But this letter would be the third one I mailed in a month, so I'm sure I'm safe within the law.

Anyway, I'll seal up the letter now, leave it on the sidewalk and start off and hope that a bus picks it up and soon after, picks me up too.

Very best,
Rudy

DEAR KEVIN!

Dear Kevin:

It seems so long since I last wrote you that I forget where I left off. It was probably somewhere on the road. Now I remember: it was Nowhere, on the sidewalk. I was heading in the direction the bus had gone when a car came along.

I stuck my thumb out for a ride. The car slowed down. Just as it got right up to me, the man sitting beside the driver grabbed my thumb and said "Step on it, Jack."

The driver stepped on it all right. I was dragged alongside the car by my thumb, yelling at this man to let me go as I only wanted a ride.

"That's what we're giving you," he said. "One ride for one thumb."

"I wasn't giving you my thumb. Just sticking it out for a hitch."

He let go of me. As the car whizzed away and I was rolling after it like a bowling ball, he shouted "And I thought you were giving me your thumb because it's my birthday today."

"Happy birthday," I yelled when I rolled to a stop. "And many more."

I wasn't that bruised and continued walking till I saw another car coming along. This one I didn't stick my thumb out for, as today might also be the birthday of the passenger or wedding anniversary of the driver. I stood on the side and out of the way of the car, in case it didn't want to stop.

But the driver swerved off his path and aimed his car at me. When I darted left, the car went left. When I shifted right, the car went right. There was no place to hide except behind the car chasing me. For a mile around there was nothing but flat sidewalk without even lampposts or signs to duck around or climb. Then I tripped. The car drove straight at me. But at the last moment it sideswiped me and came to a screeching stop.

"What are you doing standing in the middle of the sidewalk?" he said.

"What you mean is why are you driving on the sidewalk?" I said, brushing the car's paint off my clothes.

"Wise guy, I see." He put on his glasses and said "Yeah, I can really see you are a wise guy." He opened the door, emptied his ashtrays on the sidewalk and let his two dogs out to walk.

"Don't you know it's illegal to litter the sidewalk?" I said.

"I'm not littering the sidewalk, only emptying my ashtrays."

"And don't you know by now to curb your dogs?"

"Where's the curb? This burg's all sidewalk."

"Then don't you know not to let your darn dogs run loose on the sidewalk?"

"They're not darn dogs but Great Danes." He ordered them back in the car and started up the engine.

"You forgot your ashtrays," I said, holding them up.

"No thanks, I don't smoke," and he drove off.

The next car to come along I didn't hold out my thumb or even step out of the way for. I just walked with my back to it, hoping it would drive past without grazing me. But the car stopped beside me. The lady driver leaned across the front seat and said "Looking for a ride, love?"

"As a matter of fact I am. Could you give me one?"

"I don't have any today. But the car behind me stocked up all last week with them and I know he still has plenty. Tell him Jane sent you," and she drove off.

I flagged the next car down and told the driver "Jane sent me."

"Jane sends me too—whoo whoo," and he flicked his directional signals before driving off.

Maybe a sign would work. I got a sheet of paper from my typewriter case and wrote on it in big letters AIRPORT!

The next car stopped. The driver got out and so close to the sign that his nose pushed it back a few feet, and said "Oh—airport. It's dead ahead. Don't see how you could have missed it. Go left at Alley Road. Right at Avenue Street. Over the underpass. Under the overpass. Out into the bypass and bypass the bypath and go by path by the canyon pass and if you find the ferry, take the raft beneath the bridge. If you can't find the ferry, ford the stream. You can't afford the stream, take a creek. Then tear into the detour. Go roundabout through the straightaway. Poke along the speedway for five miles. Open her up on the footpath for two kilometers. Then north by southwest past the fifth tollbooth on the freeway for three furlongs and you're there."

"But I don't have a car. I was thinking of a hitch."

"Thinking's a good way to pass the time while you're hitching," and he sped off.

I waved down the next car. The driver read my sign and said "Airport? And you say it's in this direction? Thanks a lot, as I thought I was driving the wrong way."

I threw my sign away and with both hands waved down the next car.

"Can you please give me a ride," I said. "I'm desperate."

"By all means," the driver said. He lit a match and held it out for me.

"No," I said, blowing it out. "I mean a hitch. I'd like to hitch a ride in your car."

"Ah, a hitch. I knew something was up." He dropped a coin in my hand and raised his window.

"You don't understand," I said, rapping on his window. "I'm a hitchhiker, not a beggar."

"Oh, that's too bad. Do tell me what happened."

"A bus dropped me off near here and now I can't get a ride."

"By a bus, no less. My my. Close your mouth."

"What's with my mouth? You don't want to give me a ride, say so."

"I didn't say so? That's funny. In all the time I've talked to you I thought I said so at least once. Anyway, now I've certainly said so. Several times—of that I'm sure."

"Listen. All I'm asking is to get to the airport."

"Why didn't you say that in the first place?" He motioned me into the car. I sat beside him and he felt my forehead and put his ear to my chest.

"You seem unwell," he said, "which puzzles me. Lungs all clogged. Heartbeat irregular. Maybe a more thorough weigh-in at the airport will be necessary."

"I feel fine. Nothing's wrong with my body or baggage. I'm hungry, that's all."

"Me too." He patted his bloated stomach. "Very hungry. Starved is more like it. They give you too much to eat in this country."

"I wish I could say that."

"You can't say the word 'that'? I always found it one of the easiest to say. And it's your language originally, so I shouldn't be the one tutoring you. But put your tongue to the roof of your mouth like this and go 'th th' and add an 'at' and you've got 'that.' Try it."

"You want me to say the word 'it' or 'that?'"

"Now 'it' is a bit different. It's more like trying to cough something out of your throat. I don't mean the word 'it's' is said by trying to cough something out of your throat, but the word 'it.' For 'it's' you don't cough anything, but say the word 'bits' and then take off the 'b,' Well, take it off. Not the word 'it,' but the bee. It's on your jacket lapel. If you don't take it off, it'll sting your neck. And I'm not saying the word 'it'll' will sting your neck, but the bee. Though if I did want to say the word 'it'll,' I'd say 'bit' and take off the 'b' and then add a little 'ill.' And no matter what you say, you do seem to be a little ill. And you haven't yet taken off the bee."

"I don't feel ill. As I said, I feel fine, only hungry. Which no matter what you say, you don't seem to be."

"I don't seem to be, I see the bee. Still there on your jacket lapel. Then I'll take it off if you don't see the bee." He slapped at the jacket lapel. "All gone. I never even saw it come in or leave through the window. Not the word 'it' come in or leave, but the bee. Words like 'it' and 'it's' and 'bits' don't come in and leave through windows. They fly in through your ears and leave through your mouth, but only after you learn how to say them. And I of course don't mean the word 'them.' Though saying 'them' is very much like saying 'that.' The 'th th' of my first lesson—remember it? Not 'it' but 'that'? But let's start for the airport. You have to catch a plane right away?"

"First one I can get."

"Then this is your lucky day as I happen to be a pilot and am going to the airport myself. Not by myself now, of course, but with you. But let's be off."

He started to drive. I didn't know how lucky I was, but I at least finally got a ride.

After a while I said, just to make conversation, "Nice day."

"Don't I know," he said. "Terrible out. Though there'll be good days ahead, I'm afraid."

The sun was out and sky was clear and it was the prettiest day I could think of, but to him it was terrible. Okay. Some people you can never satisfy.

"Though tomorrow is supposed to get cold and nasty again," I said.

He grinned. "What did I tell you. Wonderful, no? We could use some nice weather for a change."

I realized now I was riding with a man who either had great trouble with our language or who was very strange and I should only try and amuse for the rest of the trip. So I smiled and he said "Anything wrong?"

"No, everything's terrific."

"I know, I can see it on your face. You seem to be in some pain. What is it? After all, I am a pilot."

"Honestly, it's nothing."

"Come come, you can tell me. Perhaps it's your throat from when you were trying to cough up the word 'it.' Do what I say. Close your mouth. Pull in your tongue."

"Look. You don't want me to say anything, I won't. I'll just watch you drive."

"Maybe it's all in your mind. Something I said before bother you?"

"No. I never felt better." I pounded my chest and started to whistle a happy tune.

"Please. I like a sad story as much as the next Samuel. But this has gone too far. I insist you tell me a lie."

"Wait a second. I tried to be nice till now. As I am a guest in your car and I want to get to the airport. But buster, you are very strange."

"I know, isn't that awful? It took many years of flying to get that way too. Though you don't have to be a pilot and drive actual planes to become strange. All sorts of people in every profession can get that way too. For I was once like you. A long time from now. Frowning all the time. Whistling mournful tunes. Everyone knew something was right with me but me. But you can start worrying. Because once we get to the airport, things can only get worse for you."

"That's what I'm afraid of. Stop the car and let me out."

"Exactly what I'm doing," and he drove even faster. Soon we

were off the Nowhere sidewalk and on the highway.

"I said stop the car and let me out."

"I am, I am, young man. Now get hold of yourself or you'll make my driving easier."

"You going to stop this car or not?" I yelled.

"I'm not," he said, stopping in front of a building marked Hospital. "Well, here we are. The airport."

"Airport, my foot. It says hospital."

"Hospital? I see you'll have to have your eyes weighed in too. Take my advice. What you need is an airport, not a hospital. You don't want to be running away all the time just because things get good. Put yourself in my hands. I'm Captain Wick—an experienced pilot. I've studied at the finest flying schools. Flown with the best airlines and worked under the greatest pilots in the world. I've never lost a passenger or had a serious accident. With me you can be sure you'll return safe and sound from all your flights."

He yelled to a couple of orderlies in front of the hospital. "You porters there. Help me with this passenger's bags. He has to buy a ticket and catch a plane, fast."

The orderlies grabbed me and dragged me into the hospital, though they called it an airline terminal. The lobby looked like any other hospital lobby I didn't want to be at. I started to punch the orderlies to get away.

"He seems to be more afraid of flying than I thought," the captain said. "Better fasten his seat belt for him."

They put a straightjacket on me so I couldn't move my arms. The captain slipped into a white linen jacket and took my pulse as I was wheeled to the elevator.

"On our planes," he said, "you'll be given the best accommodations an airline can afford. A first-class seat in the nonsmoking section and your own stewardess."

I suppose that meant a bed in a private room with my own oxygen tank and nurse standing by, and a medical bill later that will take me a lifetime to pay. They obviously thought I was insane. And the saner and more sensible I'd tell them I was, the madder and more incurable I'd seem to them. Who knows? Maybe to this airline, a short plane hop to Chicago meant a handful of pills down my throat to make me sleep for a night. And a nonstop round-the-world flight was to them a nest of electrical wires and plugs stuck to my head to change my way of thinking forever and make me peaceful and manageable to the end. Well, no thanks. I'm far from perfect, but I didn't want my brains and life screwed around with like that. To get out of this place, I knew I'd have to start speaking in their language right away.

"Nice place you have here," I said, when they wheeled me into my room.

"Oh, you don't like it?" Captain Wick said. "I'm happy, because we got the best baker in the state to draw up the plans."

“Really fantastic,” I said, bouncing up and down on the bed. “Especially this seat. It’s so lumpy and hard. And also the large doors. They give such a wide view of the ugly weather inside.”

Yes, it is a miserable night.” He stared out the small barred window to the clear and sunny sky. “Though very bad weather for flying. And we do seem to be disagreeing on everything at first, Miss Foy. Tell me, how do you feel?”

“Awful. Nothing hurts. Your nose, for a lot of things,” and I showed him my ear. “And this seat belt isn’t tight enough and is making my legs ache.”

“That so?”

“No,” I said.

“Oh, you really are making a great setback, old girl.”

“That’s bad, isn’t it?”

“No, it isn’t. I’ve never touched such a slow reversal before. Though it could mean you won’t have to fly with us after all. Close your mouth.”

I opened it.

“Pull back your tongue.”

I stuck out my tongue.

“Say ahhh.”

I didn’t say anything.

“Now turn around. I want to put my scalpel to your back and listen to your breathing.”

I didn’t move. He placed a stethoscope to my heart and put his eyes to the two ear plugs.

“I can’t see anything,” he said. “Are you pretending to feel worse?”

“Yes, I’m pretending.”

“You are?”

“Yes, I’m not.” I wasn’t sure what he was asking or how I should switch my words around and phrase them for him.

Because after talking to him so long I learned that some words were opposite and others just completely off. "Look, I've got to tell a lie. I never tasted so bad in my life. Left from the end. Long after I met me. I don't see how I can smell in that world inside. If I were me I wouldn't let you stay here another century, so please let me leave."

"No, it seems we'll have to keep you here after all."

He told the orderlies to unfasten my seat belt and cancel my ticket.

"It's too bad also," he said. "As I was planning an extremely rough trip to Boston for you tonight, just to get you used to flying."

"I hate you for this. As I've always hated everyone in my life."

"That's the nicest thing any passenger ever said to me. For you know, even pilots, no matter how much we earn, like to feel we're appreciated by the people we fly. Hello," he said, leaving the room.

"Hiya, captain," I yelled after him.

I was dressing to leave when the nurse brought my breakfast in. I ate it, starting with the desert first and ending with my putting the napkin on my neck and sitting down at the table. Then I began this letter. When I finish it I'll drop it in the lobby mailbox and give the airline terminal as your address. For my return address, I'll write your name and where you live in California. I'm sure that's the only way this letter will ever get to you from here. Now I'm going to erase my name at the bottom of the page, unseal the envelope flap, remove the stamps from the envelope and stick them back in my pocket, and walk backwards up the stairs and into the lobby and outside.

Most sincerely,
Rudy

Dear Kevin:

I think I discovered why there was that tremendous mix-up of language and things in my last letter.

After I left the lobby I spoke to the doorman in front of the hospital. He told me the hospital is run by and for a not-very-well-known people in America called Translibipians. He said they came from the island of Translibipia, which was once in one of the oceans near India. And that this island kept on being invaded and conquered by warriors from other islands and that the Translibipians, because of these invasions, hadn't been a free people for almost 2,000 years.

Finally, the leaders of Translibipia felt that the only way they could ever be a free people and have a free island was for them to be free of their island and their island to be free of the ocean. So one night, when the newest conquerors were asleep, all the Translibipians got aboard their fishing boats. Then the ten strongest Translibipians opened up the dams of the island. There were few trees and no hills, rocks or grass in Translibipia, and all the buildings and roads were made of sand and baked mud. In a few hours the island crumbled apart from the flooding waters and sank into the ocean.

The conquerors quickly gathered up everything they had looted, returned to their ships and steamed back to their own rich island. The Translibipians sailed in the opposite direction, for America. It seems one of the conquerors many years before had spoken of America as being "The land of the free and the home of the brave," which in their language means "The pleasant people of

Translibipia." So naturally the Translibipians believed America was also their island and had belonged to them from the start.

When they got to America they docked in the East River near the United Nations building, planted their flag on the traffic divider of the East Side Drive and declared this land to be theirs. But a city policeman ordered them to roll up their flag and go back to wherever they had come from, as there were already more than 200 million people living here called Americans.

"Well, that's you, by Zod," the Translibipian leaders said, meaning of course "That's us." "Because in your language," they said, "Americans means Translibipians."

The policeman still ordered them to sail out of the East River right away.

The Translibipians got in their boats, sailed out of the harbor and docked at the tip of the Hudson River under the Verrazano Bridge. This time they asked to be let into this country as immigrants, which in their language means "conquerors."

You see, the Translibipians were sick and tired of being slaves and captives in their own country. This time they were going to be the conquerors. But they knew little about conquering, as they had never done it before. They thought all they had to do was ask to be the conquerors of whatever island they landed on. Just as they, for 2,000 years, had always surrendered Translibipia to whatever invaders or drifters or shipwreck survivors had landed on their island and asked for it.

But American immigration officials thought the Translibipians really did want to become immigrants, as that was the word for "conquerors" they kept using. The officials asked them where they were from, as they wanted to know if the quota of immigrants allowed each year into America from that country had been filled.

"You go," the Translibipians said in their language, "to an ocean that is many feet from here and a few miles underwater."

The Americans, when they got that sentence translated, thought they had a school of talking fish on their hands and told the Translibipians to swim to the Coney Island Aquarium. There, if they performed well and the aquarium didn't already have too many of the same species of fish in their tanks, they could get plenty of food, living space and jobs. For it seems there is an American law that forbids any kind of sea animal from becoming immigrants to this country and then citizens. Though there is nothing to prevent them from working here a few years on a temporary work visa.

Eventually the Translibipians convinced the American officials that they were human beings and not some unusual kind of highly advanced sea life. The Americans then agreed to let them in as immigrants. This was fine with the Translibipians, since to them it meant that for the first time in their 2,000-year-old civilization they had become conquerors.

The doorman also said that the very day they were let into this country, they renamed the land "America" after their last island—"America" being how they said and spelled "Translibipia" in Translibipianese. They also made a new flag for their new country. It looks exactly like the one our America has. The fifty stars in their flag is a symbol for the fifty families who crossed the ocean to get here, the thirteen red and white stripes stand for the seven rough weeks and six calm weekends it took to sail across, and the blue in their flag stands for the sea and sky. Though because "sea" means "sky" in their language and "sky" means "sea," the color blue might mean something different to them.

The doorman told me there are lots of other words which look and sound like our words, but which mean something else in Translibipianese. For instance, the word "ocean" in English means and is spelled "island" in Translibipianese, and vice versa.

And the word "woman" means and is spelled "man" in Translibipianese, and vice versa. In fact, "versa" means "vice" in their language, and vice versa or versa vice—whichever language you prefer to use.

If you haven't a big interest in languages as I do, then you should probably skip all this. I find it fascinating that so many Translibipianese words mean the exact opposite in English, though the word "Translibipianese" doesn't mean "English." It means "Americanese." "English" in their language means "Russian." And "Russian" means "Chinese." And "Chinese" means "dungarees." But to say the English words "My dungarees" in Translibipianese, you say "Your long red sneeze." And to say the English words "My first pair of Russian dungarees," you say "Your long clean triple red Chinese sneeze."

As you can tell, you can't learn their language just by finding the opposite or near-opposite word in English and then think that word will be Translibipianese. For instance, the one word "word" in English means the word "opposite" in Translibipianese, and vice versa. But the two words "one word" in English means the two words "two words" in Translibipianese, and vice versa. While the two words "two words" in English mean the two words "three words" in their language. And so on and so forth as we say in English, which in Translibipianese means "These clever tootsies are always one number ahead of us in their language," something the Translibipians are very proud of.

This language confusion almost never ends, I learned. Though sometimes I can honestly say their language makes more sense than ours. For instance, our word "honestly" means "untruthfully" in their language, and vice versa. And "confusion" means "clearness" in their language, and our "I learned" means both "not sure" and "don't know." But our "sense" means "nonsense" in their language and they have no word for "sense." "For instance" means and sounds and is spelled the same in both languages, even though they've never seen or heard any English words other than that one sentence I mentioned before: "The land of the free and the home of the brave."

That sentence they heard from an American messboy. He'd been heaved over the side of his ship for spilling a bowl of cereal on his officer, and landed on the sands of Translibipia on a wooden raft. The boy was only ten years old when he landed and very thin from not having eaten anything for weeks but the bark and wood of his raft. He'd eaten so much of the raft that by the time he reached Translibipia, he only had half a log left to float in on. But still—alone and weak as he was— the first thing he demanded after he pointed to himself and said "Land of the free and home of the brave," was to be the sole ruler and owner of Translibipia. And like all the castaways before him who had made the same demand, he was quickly given the island.

But let me get back to the Translibipian hospital. Or as they would say: An American airport.

I still don't know why there was such a large hospital for so few Translibipians here. I suppose their hospital needs are much greater than ours. I know their cures are much different. The doorman said that when a patient comes in for a simple toothache, the doctors operate on one of his toes. If it's the front teeth that hurt, they operate on the big toes. If it's any of the other teeth or one of his eyeballs, they stuff up the patient's nose with his pinkies and operate on one of his smaller toes. Now if it's only a headache the patient has, the Translibipian cure is for three orderlies to pick up a glass of water, two aspirins and a doctor and throw them all against a wall.

I could have talked to that doorman all day he was so interesting. But I wanted to get moving again to Palo Alto, so I said goodbye.

"I'm fine, thanks," he said, "for I only work here. But how are you?"

"I'm sorry. I of course meant to say hello."

"Oh, that's wrong. I forgot you're a Translibipian. Then hello," and he shook my earlobe, waved for me to come to him and went into the hospital.

I stood outside and thought I'd already tried taking a cab, bus, hitching and getting to the airport, so maybe the best way would be by train.

I walked to the train station and looked around for a ticket window. I saw one open, ducked around it and ran down the ramp to the platform and got on the baggage car of a train going to San Francisco.

I thought I'd squat down like a suitcase, with one hand hidden in my jacket and the other curled up on top of my head to resemble a handle. But the baggage car was already filled with lots of children and adults pretending to be trunks and overnight bags, and whole families bunched together to look like large crates.

I went to the mail car. Nothing was inside it but bags of letters and bundles of magazines and ads. I squatted on the floor pretending to be a package of books going by fourth-class mail to Palo Alto.

I woke up when the door of the mail car was slammed open. Some men dumped all the mail and me into a waiting truck and drove us to the main post office in Columbus, Ohio.

One of the men sorting the mail in the post office picked me up and said "This package just off the train has no address on it, Sid. What do I do?"

"You're new here," Sid said, "right?"

"Yeah, new," the man said.

"I can tell. I never saw you before and you asked mo a question when you didn't know what to do. Well, you first drop the package on the floor like this. No, don't worry, it's only books. They can't break except for the spines a little. Now you do this to see if the package is wrapped right and the books don't fall out."

"And they didn't," the man said.

"Right. So we're getting somewhere with this package. What you next want to find out is the address. To do that, you kick the package around the floor a little. You know—a little boot here and a solid kick there. Just like I'm doing. But no harder, unless you want to be buying a new pair of shoes every month. This time it's not to find out if the package is wrapped right that we're kicking it. Or even to make the package torn and useless like sore postal workers say we should do to packages that give us a hard time. No, it's to see if maybe the address sticker will fall out of the creases in the wrapping."

"But none did."

"Right again," Sid said. "You got sharp eyes. Like you saw right away there was no address on the package. And then that it didn't fall apart when I dropped it. That's good. Keep thinking like that and you'll be going places in this office."

"What do we do next?"

"Look at you. All hot to go. I like that. Means you just don't want to sit around doing nothing all day like the rest of the gang here. Well, next you hold the package over a low flame. You do this to see if the address was written in invisible ink that only comes out under a flame. But you never let the flame get too close to the wrapping, or what do you think will happen?"

"The flame will get snuffed out?"

"The package will burn."

"Oh yeah. Because there are books inside."

"Because the wrapping is made of paper."

"Of course. I forgot. Did the address come out from the flame?"

"I thought I said you got sharp eyes. Because nothing came out on the package wrapping but a lot of red marks all around.

That means the address wasn't written in any kind of invisible ink that we know how to make appear. So next you toss the package in the air a few times and catch it like this. Well, I dropped it. So if the package turns out to be too heavy to catch, you get another worker to help you toss it up and catch it like I want you to do with me. Now it's important you throw it higher and higher each time. But after the fourth toss and catch, you toss it high as you can and try to get it to land flat on this table in front of the mail chute. We got it to land on the table, but not flat. So we have to keep tossing it just as high till it does land the right way in front of the chute. Now the reason we're doing this is to see if the address that couldn't be kicked out of the wrapping before will come out this way."

"And it didn't."

"That's right, it didn't. So now you got to give up on ever finding where this package is going. As there's a post-office rule that you're only allowed to do so much in trying to find the address on a package, before you just have to stamp it and shove it down the chute with the other unaddressed mail. Break this rule once—just once—and I swear I'll see that you never work in a post office again. Because we don't keep anyone on here who horses around and doesn't stick to the rules and moves the mail right, understand?"

"Got ya," the man said. He stamped on my forehead RETURN TO NEW YORK: NO ADDRESS GIVEN, and pushed me down the chute into the basement.

I was put in a mail bag there with a lot of other unaddressed packages. The bag was locked at the top and flung into a truck, which drove to the train station. Then my bag was dumped into the mail car and the train soon began moving.

I've been writing this letter from inside the mail bag. A few packages from some of the other bags in the car just yelled for me

to pipe down with my typing as it's keeping them awake. Maybe these packages have a lot of room in their bags and can stretch out and fall asleep with ease. But my bag is filled to the top and very uncomfortable, so I know I'll be twisting and tossing around inside it all night.

Anyway, the right thing to do is to stop typing so these other packages can get some sleep. I wish you well and hope to see you soon.

Rudy

Dear Kevin:

The mail bag I was in landed in New York, was brought to the main post office on 33rd Street, and with the rest of the bags I came in on the train with, left in a room for two days. Then I got the brainstorm to feel inside the other packages in my bag. If something sharp was in one of them, I'd use it to cut my way out.

Someone, I discovered, was sending a jackknife through the mail. I hope the person expecting the knife didn't know he was getting one, because that's the something sharp I used to slice open my bag.

I climbed out and said to the 200 or so other bags piled on top of one another with my bag being a few from the top, "Hey? Any package in one of the bags want to be let out?"

"I kind of like it in here," a voice said from one of the bottom bags.

"I don't," another voice said from the same bag.

"You two want to be let out or not?" I said.

"No."

"Yes."

"Look," the first voice said to the other. "I promise no more arguing. And that I'll stop smoking in here and won't hog most of the room when we sleep. And lastly, that I won't fool around with any other package in the bag but you."

"Okay then," the second voice said. "We stay."

Well, I didn't want to hang around and get involved in any more arguments between two packages in a bag and maybe get caught by a post-office worker. And then stored away in the

Address Unknown section here till I was either claimed by the person who mailed me or auctioned off as a package of books in the post office's annual sale of unclaimed mail. So I climbed down the pile to the grunts and groans of the bags I was stepping on, and slipped past the working part of the post office into the customer's section. Then to avoid any suspicion that I was a package escaping from the post office, I quickly pretended to be a customer on the stamp line.

This was much easier to pretend to be, as I look more like a stamp customer than a package of books. Though as a package of

books I didn't need to have money on me, which is probably why I wasn't recognized as a person by so many postal workers for the past few days. While on line I needed money for whatever it is a person pretending to be a stamp customer might have to buy.

"Next," the clerk said behind the stamp counter.

"Um, let's see," I said. "I'd like one of something. Two of another thing. Three of anything else I might want. And maybe one more thing besides."

"Will you hurry it up?" a customer said behind me. "There are twenty people on line."

"Cancel that order," I told the clerk. "Instead I'll have three more of some other thing. Two less of a few more things. Definitely one each of anything I haven't asked for yet. And if it's no bother, nothing else I forgot besides."

"I'm afraid they're all out of everything you want to buy today," the customer behind me said. "Next," she shouted into my ear and shoved me off the line.

"I'd like one nine cent stamp with my face on it," the clerk said to her, "and three picture postcards."

"We only sell the cards plain," she said to him.

"Not even with butter on them? A little mayonnaise? Because I hate to have my cards dry."

She reached through his stamp window, spilled his coffee cup on the postcards, took some change he had in front of him for his postage money and said "Next."

"I'd like the same thing the clerk just ordered," the customer behind the woman said to her, "but with less cream on my cards."

I mailed the last letter I wrote you and left the building.

A parade was passing in front of the post office when I got outside. I'd never been in a parade, so didn't know where they all ended once they were through. Maybe all the parades I'd seen in the past ended in Palo Alto. Or if they only marched across the country and ended in San Francisco, then from there I might be able to join a new parade marching through Palo Alto on its way to New York. But the only way to find out where they all ended was to join one. I leaped over the police barricade and got behind a high-school band. Because I had no instrument, I opened my typewriter case and typed on the keys with one hand.

We marched to Fifth Avenue. Up to 81st Street. Through the Metropolitan Museum of Art and out its back entrance into Central Park. Then through the park to 110th Street. Right to Madison. Down Madison to 42nd Street and over to the main branch of

the public library, which we marched around three times before the parade ended and the band and all the marchers packed their instruments and guns and flags and floats and started home.

“Good parade,” a drum majorette said. “And you type very well. What schools you go to for it?”

“None. I type by ear.”

“Pity. Because I’m sure if you had taken lessons for a few years, you’d be typing on a concert stage by now. Well, see you in the next parade,” and she threw in the air the box her baton was in, caught it behind her back, twirled it under her legs, and bouncing the box from one knee to the other, high-stepped away.

I sat on the library steps and thought that I had used up all the ways to get to Palo Alto that I knew of. But as long as I was in front of one of the world's largest book collections, I should go inside and see if they have a travel book on how to get to Palo Alto.

The man at the library's information booth told me to go to the Palo Alto room to find what I was looking for. In the Palo Alto room I asked the librarian if she had a book dealing with every possible way to get to Palo Alto.

"But you are in Palo Alto," she said, holding a handkerchief over her nose because of what she feared was the heavy smog drifting up from Southern California and settling over Palo Alto today.

"I mean the city of Palo Alto, not the room."

"Excuse me. I've been around all these Palo Alto books so long that I feel I'm living there sometimes. But why go to Palo Alto when you can learn much more about it from reading here?"

"I've a good friend there I want to see. Kevin Wafer."

"Kevin, Kevin. No, I don't know him personally. But I'll get you his book and save you the cost and time of a trip there. We keep all our biographies up-to-date. If he's not too old, he won't take you long to read. What street is he on?"

"Leary. But I want to see him, not read about him."

"Nonsense. Now sit down. Make yourself at home. Like me to build a fire? And don't split on me, man, and I'll bring you Kevin's groovy book and a sweet roll and sody pop. I mean, don't leave, sir, and I'll bring his nice book and a danish pastry and bottle of soda."

She climbed the bookshelf ladder and rolled along on it till she came to the shelf marked Leary Street. She counted off the first letters of people's last names on the shelf till she got to W, then began reading their names.

"Wackamaw... Wackaslaw... Wacky... Wackydup... Waddle... Waddles... Wafawin... Wafelost... Wafer. Here it is."

She pulled a book out and brought it over. It had your name on the cover and a recent photo of you on the first page. Inside the book were lots of facts about your life. All the facts, in fact. Starting with the first facts of where and when you were born and who was under the football-stadium stands when it happened and what each member of both football teams said when they jogged out of the dressing room to the field and saw you. And then all the places you've lived in or traveled to after that. Your schools, teachers, friends, classmates, toys you've owned and clothes you've worn and foods you've liked or disliked or once liked and then didn't like and now like again. Even your favorite color and ice-cream flavor and lucky number and all the dreams and nightmares you woke up remembering and imaginings and wishes you went to sleep with or dozed off in class thinking about. Even a list of all the funny and intelligent things you said. And another list with side-by-side snapshots of all the persons and animals you met and drawings and constructions you made and birthday cakes you had and holiday trees you helped decorate. And even a tiny mention of me when for a while I lived with you and your mom and dog till about a year ago.

"You keep searching through that," she said, "while I hunt up your ways to get to Palo Alto book."

Other than for most of your dreams and wishes and things, your book didn't tell me much about you I didn't already know. Except that your first words were "Doctor, you look exquisite tonight," while I thought they were "Will you stop twiddling around with my nose, you clumsy oaf." And that nobody thought you old enough to walk when you kissed your dog goodbye at the door, crawled after the bus at the corner, and lifted yourself up and stepped to the rear of the bus as the driver had ordered.

"Success," the librarian shouted from the top rung of the ladder. She stood up straight waving a book and banged her head on the ceiling, climbed down with the *Ways to Get to Palo Alto Book* and set it before me.

"In going to Palo Alto," I read, "avoid nowhere."

So this book might be of some use to me after all, I thought.

"Get on the front of a three-legged horse," I read, "and you'll be riding two steps backwards all the way."

"Now that's a lot of help," I said. "What is this you gave me—the *Palo Alto Book of Riddles*?"

"Why? Want me to get you that book too?"

Just then a man ran into the room and said "Quick hurry fast. It's almost too fast. Maybe it is too late. Because do you have the *Palo Alto Book of Riddles*?"

"I was just about to fetch it for Mr. Foy," she told him.

"No no no. Quick fast hurry. I mean quick hurry fast. As I've tried all the new bookstores. Looked through all the old bookshops. They all told me I had to buy a book called the *How to Find the Palo Alto Book of Riddles Book* to find the *Palo Alto Book of Riddles*. But that *How to Find the Palo Alto Book of Riddles Book* was too expensive to buy. I first had to buy a cheaper book called the *How to Find and Hold a Job for a Week Book* to find and hold a job for a week so I could afford the *How to Find the Palo Alto Book of Riddles Book*. But to pay for the *How to Find and Hold a Job for a Week Book*, I first had to find, hold and quit a job after a day with a day's pay. So I borrowed my friend's *How to Find, Hold and Quit a Job after a Day with a Day's Pay Book*. I read it. Found, held and quit a job after a day with a day's pay, and with that money bought the *How to Find and Hold a Job for a Week Book*. Read it. Found and held a job for a week and got paid a week's wage for my work and went back to the bookstore to buy the *How to Find the Palo Alto Book of Riddles Book*.

But the price of that book had gone up twenty percent in a week. So I again had to borrow my friend's *How to Find, Hold and Quit a Job after a Day with a Day's Pay Book*. Read it. Found, held and quit another job after a day with another day's pay and now had enough money to buy the *How to Find the Palo Alto Book of Riddles Book*. It turned out to be a hundred blank pages, except for the two middle ones. These two pages had scrawled across them 'To find the *Palo Alto Book of Riddles*, go to the Palo Alto room of the New York 42nd Street Library between the minutes of 2:15 and 2:18 pm on a windy day in a "J" month. Now,' the scrawl continued, 'can you satisfactorily answer these four questions? Two, is the riddles book still worth getting? Three, was it really worth all this trouble to get? And four, why couldn't you figure out for yourself how to get the *Palo Alto Book of Riddles* without working so hard and paying such a ridiculously high price for the *How to Find the Palo Alto Book of Riddles Book* and buying and borrowing those other books?'"

"Was it all worth it?" I said.

"No, because I still can't answer the four questions except for the third one which I'm answering now. Though fortunately the scrawl didn't say that if I couldn't answer the questions, I couldn't get the *Palo Alto Book of Riddles*. But here I am. Is it too late? Don't tell me it is, as that will waste even more time. Because fast hurry quick. I mean quick hurry fast. As it's 2:17 and forty seconds, so I only have twenty seconds left. Now only fifteen seconds left. Now only twelve. Now eight. For time's flying and wind's dying and if we wait too long it won't even be a 'J' month."

I told the librarian to give him the riddles book. He thanked me and looked over my shoulder at the book I was reading.

"Oh, the *Ways to Get to Palo Alto Book*," he said. "I read it. Very exciting and dull, don't you think? I especially liked the ending. So much like the beginning. Or is it the middle section

I'm thinking of now and the beginning was like the end? And so quick to read and slow. And that part with the three-legged horse still makes me happy and sad."

"What do you make of that three-legged horse?" I said.

"I don't know. All the answers to the problems in the *Ways to Get to Palo Alto Book* are in this riddles book. I always forget what I read, but love having the tougher parts explained. So a big 'Yes' I can finally answer to all four of those questions in the *How to Find the Palo Alto Book of Riddles Book*. It is worth it. It was worth it. I never could have figured out for myself how to get the *Palo Alto Book of Riddles* without buying and borrowing those other books. And I can satisfactorily answer these four questions.

"But that part of the *Ways to Get to Palo Alto Book* you're now reading?" he said. "When the traveler gets trapped in that house with many rooms? So real and unreal. Or is it a mountain with many mountains inside that the traveler gets trapped in? Or are all those mountains inside one room? But I do remember how scared and brave I was when I read it. Which reminds me, I must leave right now. I'm afraid of library rooms. Or any kind of libraries or rooms. For as I say: 'Many doors, too few throughs, and windows aren't enough.'"

"What's that mean?" I said.

"Beats me. Sentence I read in your *Ways to Get to Palo Alto Book*. Though all the answers are in my riddles book, which you can borrow when I'm done."

"How long will that be?"

"Answer to that one is in my riddles book too."

He asked the librarian how to get out of the Palo Alto room.

"Read page forty-two, line six of the *Palo Alto Book of Riddles*," she said.

He turned to page forty-two and read aloud "'Leave through the one door.' Good," he said, "I'm going," and left.

I opened my *Ways to Get to Palo Alto Book* to the "Tips to Travelers" section.

"In going to Palo Alto," I read, "avoid sitting on a log. If you can't avoid sitting on a log, try not to sit on one too hard. If you must sit on one too hard, don't sit on it at all. If you must sit on it at all, avoid going to Palo Alto. If you can't avoid going to Palo Alto, go to a different one. If there isn't a different Palo Alto, build one. If you can't build one, build two. If you can't build two, have someone build them for you. If you can't find someone to build them for you, have him build them for someone else. If he builds them for someone else, don't have him build them with logs. If he must build them with logs, avoid sitting on one. If you can't avoid sitting on a log, start reading from the second part of the second sentence of this paragraph."

I skipped a few pages to the section titled "Station Wagons."

"Once a day," I read, "a station wagon leaves for Palo Alto from the Station Wagon Station. Tickets may be bought at the Station Wagon Station ticket office. Lower fares for passengers willing to share driving. Higher fares for drivers willing only to be passengers. No fares for people not willing to be passengers or drivers."

That's for me, I thought. "So long," I said to the librarian, who seemed to have disappeared. "And thanks very much."

"Oh Mr. Foy," she said. "Yoo-hoo, Mr. Foy. I'm way up here." She was on a bookshelf ladder on the third balcony, speaking to me through a megaphone and waving what looked like a book. "I found another copy of the *Palo Alto Book of Riddles*, Mr. Foy. Pages are yellow and torn. A rare first edition. Written by hand in the original language of the California Indians who first plotted the route centuries ago and wrote the book. If you found a very old California Indian along the way to teach you their language and sew up the pages, this book could be of some use."

"No time. Station wagon is about to go."

I ran down the library steps and across town to the Station Wagon Station ticket office. It was in room 302 of an office building.

I got on the elevator and pressed button "3" for the third floor. Three fans in the elevator went on. The doors closed. Lights began blinking on and off. Dance music from a wall speaker started to play. But the elevator didn't move.

I pressed button "4" thinking I'd take the elevator to the fourth floor and walk down a flight to room 302. The doors opened and closed four times. Lights went out and the fans stopped. Music changed to an announcer giving today's traffic report.

The elevator started bumping to the basement, but got stuck between floors.

I thought I'd better get back to the lobby and walk the two flights to the third floor. I pressed button L for Lobby. The lights came back on. Small fires broke out in the fans. The doors fell off and caved in against the elevator walls. A voice on the speaker said "Lelelator lot lorking. Luse lairlase lease. Lhank lou... Lelelator lot lorking. Luse lairlase lease. Lhank lou..."

I climbed onto the elevator railing, blew the fires out and pressed button "B" for the basement, as the elevator was still stuck between floors.

The button box blew up. The floor started to give way. I held onto the railing as the floor dropped out and crashed in the basement. The voice on the speaker said "Blease bleave belebator. Blast bannoucebent. Blease bleave belebator. Blast bannouncebent."

I climbed through the trapdoor in the ceiling and out of the elevator shaft into the lobby. I walked to the third floor and went to room 302.

"Is this the Station Wagon Station ticket office?" I asked a man there.

"No, Fender and Bumper Bumper and Fender Company. How do you do? I'm Bumper. Fender's in back. Office you want is in room 812."

I climbed the five flights to room 812.

The painter painting the empty room 812 told me to go to room 509 of the building next door.

The secretary in room 509 said "The ticket office? Gosh, they moved a couple years ago to the new tall building around the block."

I went around the block. The building she spoke about hadn't been built yet. I asked a man in the one-story rental office there if he knew where the Station Wagon Station ticket office was.

He opened the blueprints for the 140-story building his company was going to put up in three years and flipped through the prints to page 126.

"Here's your ticket office," he said, pointing to one of 200 tiny boxes that will make up the 200 offices on the 126th floor. "Great view of the city also, when there aren't too many clouds below. And sometimes on the same day they'll be able to see Canada, half of America and the larger ocean liners two days out to sea. And round-the-clock evacuation teams for the tenants during the heavier storms. Special radio communication with local airports so they'll have instant alerts when planes are flying too low. Sound good? An office you always dreamed of? The crown of a working lifetime and what no great company should be without? Then what about you renting one on the 126th floor? We've only eighty offices left on that floor and no more than 12,000 left in the rest of the building. All you need is an okay from our doctors that you don't go crackers from very high altitudes or get severe nose bleeds or fainting spells from the high-speed elevator rides."

"I don't need an office for what I do."

"Then rent one just for the kick of the elevator rides. Up and down. What do we care? They're all automatic, so bring your friends with you and ride them as much as you like."

I told him I could hardly pay for the rent on my cheap apartment, and he suddenly looked cross and showed me the door.

"Yes, a very nice door you have here also," I said, rubbing and knocking on it. "Very sturdy. Good finish. Will the doorbells in your new office building be just as well made?"

I left and sat on the stoop across the street. A woman came out the door behind me and said "Now here looks like a young fellow who's got a mean itch to get to Palo Alto."

"How'd you know?"

"A little birdie told me." On her shoulder was a small bird

who never stopped talking into her ear, even when she was telling me this.

"I got just the plane ticket to get you there," she said. She reached into her pocketbook. The bird pecked her temple to get her attention and flapped his wings very fast as if what he was saying was very important.

"So sorry," she said. "But the little birdie just told me a man down the street wants to get to Palo Alto even more than you."

She got on her bike with the bird on her shoulder and pedaled to a man sitting on the curb.

"Now you look like a man who wants to get to Palo Alto real bad," she said to him.

"I can't tell you how much," he said.

"You don't have to, as the little birdie just did that."

She gave him a plane ticket to San Francisco. A helicopter ticket from the San Francisco airport to Palo Alto. And enough money for cab rides from here to Kennedy Airport and from the Palo Alto heliport to the house on Leary Street where this man wanted to go.

"Leary Street?" I said. "That's Kevin's block." I asked him what number. It was the house next to yours.

"Could you also give me a plane and helicopter ticket to San Francisco and Palo Alto?" I asked the woman. "I'll travel with this man. That way you'll save on my cab rides from here to the airport and from the heliport to Leary Street. And I won't insist the cabby also pull up in front of Kevin's house, I'll get out at this man's house next door and walk the rest of the way."

All this time the bird was talking excitedly into her ear.

"Hold it," she said to me. "I can't hear the little birdie over your chatter. Now what's that you said, birdie? No. You don't say. That's unbelievable. Thanks, sweetlife. Know what the little birdie just told me? That there's a young lady uptown who wants to get to Palo Alto in an even worse way than you two guys put together. Sorry, but I guess she's the one who gets to go."

She snatched back the tickets and cab fare from the man, got on the bike with the bird on her shoulder and rode away.

"Hey lady," I yelled. "Let us try to prove to you that put together this man and I want to get to Palo Alto even more than that girl."

"*Dumbkofs*," the bird yelled back to us.

"Well, what do you know?" the woman said. "That's the first word in English this little birdie's ever spoke."

That's when I gave up on getting to Palo Alto. After I finish this letter I'm going straight home. I suppose a nice thing for you to do would be to tell the people next door that there's a man in New York who wants to get there even more than I do. But then I don't see how they can know how much I want to see you, unless they have a little birdie of their own. Or the bird the lady has flies out to tell them before this letter arrives.

Anyway, bye for now. And no matter what the birdie tells you if it does fly out there, you'll never know how sorry I am that I couldn't get to Palo Alto. But quite honestly, getting there turned out to be much too tough a problem for me.

Very best,
Rudy

Dear Kevin:

Right after mailing you that last letter, I went home. But my home didn't seem to be my apartment anymore, as my keys didn't fit the locks and my door knocker was gone and there was now a bell.

I knocked on the bell. A man said through the peephole on the door "I'm sorry. But we don't buy anything, sell anything, want or need anything or want to need, sell or buy anything too."

"Excuse me," I said. "But if I'm not mistaken, this is my apartment."

"You're not mistaken. It is my apartment."

"Is this 5C?"

"It is."

"The apartment 5C on the fifth floor between apartments 5B and 5D at 7 West 73rd Street?"

"That's the address."

"And this building number 7 is still on the same plot of land it was on two weeks ago? Or has the foundation been tampered with and the building been removed?"

"I do sleep a great deal," he said, "and very soundly. But I'm sure this building hasn't been removed."

"Has the number of the building or floor or the apartment letter been changed recently? Or the street direction switched from West 73rd to East?"

"No."

"Then it must be the wrong city I'm in. Is this New York City?"

"That's the one."

"The New York City that's in New York State?"

"Let me check my driver's license for that. Yes, the license is for New York State. So this must be the New York City you want in that state."

"The New York State that's in the United States?"

"I'm sure that's right."

"You realize I'm now speaking about the United States that's on the continent of North America. And which has parts of the world's two largest oceans on either side of it. And lots of little lands around it called islands and waters inside it called rivers, lakes and streams."

"I'm not an expert on geography or oceanography," he said. "But I think everything you said just now indicates that we're talking about the same United States in North America."

"Then maybe the North America continent with my apartment 5C is in a different hemisphere."

"Since our Western Hemisphere is the only hemisphere in the world with a North America continent on it, then this has to be that one."

"Then maybe the Western Hemisphere with my 5C on it is no longer on the same planet it was on when I was last in my apartment."

"We're both now talking about planet Earth?" he said.

"The very same. The one that goes around the sun and has a moon called Moon and right now is closer to planet Venus than it is to Mars."

"Well, I've been listening to the radio all day. And if either one of the two hemispheres left planet Earth, I'm sure one of the news reports would have mentioned it."

"Maybe the Earth with my apartment 5C left the solar system. Did any of the news reports say anything about that?"

"Not a word. Even if I didn't hear of it on the radio or even read it in the paper, I'm sure I would have seen some kind of actual physical change taking place in the sky if our one and only planet Earth suddenly switched over to another solar system."

"Maybe the solar system which has my apartment 5C on it switched to another galaxy."

"Now a change like that I'm sure I would have known about before you knocked on my bell. If not through the radio, TV, newspaper or with my own eyes, then someone would have stopped by or at least phoned to tell me of such an event. Because since our solar system has always been part of the same Milky Way galaxy as far back as anyone can tell, that, sir, would be news."

"No. I'm sure that must be the case," I said.

"Let's say it was. And the solar system which has your apartment 5C on it had changed to another galaxy. Your 5C would still be on the same spot on earth it was always on, except billions of light years away from where Earth once revolved in its solar system."

"Then the only answer left is that the galaxy which has my apartment 5C in it is no longer part of the same universe. Or never was part of this universe, but has all the same names of streets and countries and planets and stuff of your universe. And that's how I got fouled up in trying to find the right address."

"Now there you might have a point. Maybe in your travels you made a right when you should have made a left, and got lost and somehow found your way into another universe with all the same names of apartments and planets and galaxies of your own universe. But as far as this universe is concerned, apartment 5C of 7 West 73rd Street, New York City and State, United States, North America, Western Hemisphere, planet Earth, solar system, Milky Way galaxy, is mine."

"I don't know," I said. "Somehow the idea of our two universes looking exactly alike except for your apartment having a doorbell when mine had a knocker still doesn't seem possible. I better see the landlord."

"When you do, give him this check for my next month's rent."

He stuck a check through the peephole. It was made out to the same man for the same rent that I used to pay for my apartment 5C in my universe.

The landlord lived in a second-floor apartment just like the one mine lived in. Except this landlord also had a doorbell instead of a knocker, so maybe this was a different universe I was in after all.

I rapped on the bell. He opened the door and said "Mr. Foy, How nice to see you again."

"You're probably mistaken," I said. "There's no doubt another Rudy Foy in your universe who looks just like me."

"Oh no, Mr. Foy. Mr. Brin of 5C phoned to say you were coming and that I should clear up some problems for you. First of all, all the door knockers in the building were removed a week ago when I had doorbells put in. I saved your door knocker, as I thought you might have grown attached to it after a year."

He gave me a door knocker. It looked like the old knocker on my 5C door. Though who's to say that two door knockers in two universes couldn't be made by two different door-knocker companies with the same name and then be worn down exactly alike too. That didn't seem too out of the question when I thought of the coincidences so far that everything else in this universe has looked, acted and been called the same thing in mine.

"Secondly," he said. "You haven't lost your way and wound up in another universe. You just didn't pay your last three months' rent in this universe. So I had you evicted a day after you left and rented your apartment to the Brins."

"That's absolutely and totally and without further question absurd. Because you can't have me thrown out of my apartment when I'm not there. And no matter which universe I've been in for the past two weeks, I know I haven't been in any apartment 5C in either of them since I left. I'll just take this matter up with the courts."

"I had the Courts evicted the same day as you for also not paying their rent."

"Then I'll go to the mayor's office to fight my eviction."

"The Mayors adopted a baby while you were gone and converted their office into a nursery."

"Then I'll get a lawyer. We both know there are at least two of them in this building alone."

"A Mr. Barry Lawyer on the ground floor and a Ms. Mary Lawyer in the store in front. They're unrelated though."

"I thought she was an Unrelated before she married another Mr. Lawyer and had her name changed."

"She could have been. But no matter how many lawyers you see, you'll never get your apartment back."

I went to Mr. Barry Lawyer's office on the ground floor. He said he'd take my case, but only for money.

"Why should I give you money to take my case?" I said. "Because not only would you then have my case, but I wouldn't have anything to carry my typewriter and papers in."

"Then go peddle your case somewhere else. It isn't worth anything to me anyway."

I went to the store in front of this building where Ms. Mary Unrelated Lawyer had her office. She said "I'd take your case for nothing, Mr. Foy, as I believe you were evicted illegally. But I have so many other cases to take care of first. There are the Henry Cases and Bernard Cases and Judith Case and Simon and Susan Case and all their little Cases. I'm truly sorry."

I knew I'd never get back in my apartment now, so the only thing to do was hit the road. But there are no roads in this part of the city, only streets and avenues. So I went to South Road in Central Park and hit it with my fists till my hands hurt. While I was hitting the road I kept telling myself how dumb I was for not having sent the landlord my three months' rent, even if I didn't have the money.

I also felt that because I couldn't pay for a hotel and didn't know anyone well enough to live with in New York, I might as well try to get to California again. You're the one person I know who'd put me up till I made enough money to rent a place of my own.

Best, Rudy

Dear Kevin:

After I typed and mailed that last letter, I went right back to hitting the road with my fists. But I soon realized I was getting nowhere by hitting the road, so I began hitting the bicycle path instead. But nothing came from hitting the bicycle or bridle paths either, as I still hadn't found a way to get to California with only five cents and change in my pockets and a typewriter and door knocker in my typewriter case. So I began hitting the park benches and footbridges and road signs and trees and hills and daffodils coming up and rain coming down. But nothing came from hitting any of these things.

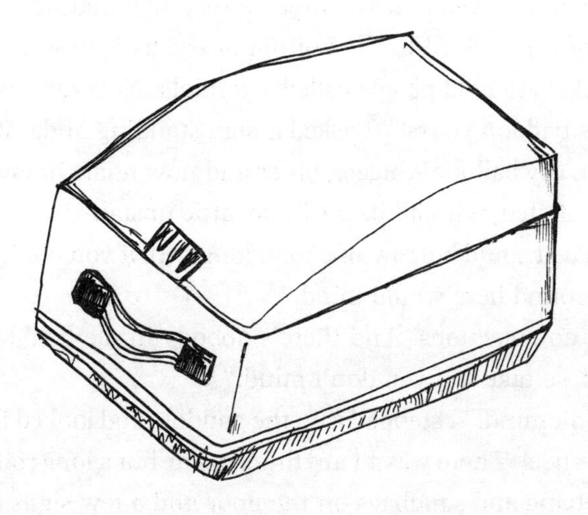

So I next began hitting myself. I hit my feet and arms and chest and then my face, but real hard, as I was getting more and more anxious to get to California. You know: slapping and socking my face back and forth and up and down and to and fro and fro and to and to fro to and fro fro to fro to, till I really laced one into my chin and knocked myself out.

A girl woke me up by throwing a glass in my face. She said she had planned to throw a glass of water in my face, but got thirsty before she reached me, so she only threw the glass.

"And I saw you fighting with yourself before," she said. "You put up a good battle, but I think you lost."

"You mean I won. As I did knock myself to the ground."

"But I counted you out on the ground. I can't count to ten myself as they do with boxers in the ring, so I counted the number nine ten times."

She helped me up and ran off with the pieces of glass. I was about to knock myself out again and maybe this time bite and kick myself as well, when I saw a balloon bobbing above the trees in a nearby field.

The balloon was at least three stories high and held to the ground by ropes. Tied to the bottom of the balloon was one of those baskets to hold people called a gondola. Nobody was in it.

"This balloon yours?" I asked a man standing under it.

"Nah. My balloon's bigger, bluer and now home in my basement uninflated, with all its air in my attic upstairs."

"Maybe I could borrow this for a long trip, if you don't think anyone around here would mind."

"I've no objections. And there's nobody in the field but the two of us, so take it if you don't mind."

"I don't mind." I stepped into the gondola and looked for the steering wheel. There wasn't anything inside but a long rolled-up balloon string and sandbags on the floor and a few signs nailed to the sides giving driving advice, such as "STAY TO THE RIGHT OF THE SKY WHEN PASSING" and "RISING MORE THAN 55 MILES PER HOUR IS PUNISHABLE BY LOSS OF BALLOONIST LICENSE FOR UP TO TWO YEARS."

I asked the man to untie the ropes. He wished me a "Bon ballonage." As the balloon started to rise, a man and boy ran to where the balloon had just taken off from.

"Poppa, poppa," the boy said. "Someone's stealing the balloon you bought me at the zoo today."

Sure enough, on the balloon were written the words CENTRAL PARK ZOO. Though there could have been hundreds of other such balloons sold at the zoo today, I figured this one had to be the boy's because of the big fuss he was putting up.

"Hold tight, kid," I shouted. "I didn't know it was yours and I'll bring it right down."

I dropped several sandbags over the side of the gondola. I thought if I was going to land this balloon, I didn't want it coming down too hard because of the weight of all that sand. But the balloon was now rising even faster.

"The string, the string, you fool," the father yelled. "Throw it over the side so we can pull the balloon down."

I threw this very long string over the side. It reached just a few inches above the father's fingers. By the time he lifted the boy to his shoulders to grab the string, the string had risen a few inches above the boy's fingers. By the time the man got on top of the boy's shoulders who was still on his father's shoulders, the string was out of reach of the man's fingers too.

They called over an elderly lady and were helping her climb up past the father and boy to the man's shoulders, when a strong breeze blew the balloon out of the park and knocked their human totem pole over. The balloon sailed across the West Side of Manhattan and over the Hudson River and New Jersey and then into some clouds.

I couldn't see anything but clouds in these clouds and a little above me, an occasional small plane or immense bird, but I hoped I was still sailing west. When the balloon passed out of the clouds above the Pittsburgh airport, I saw a large sign painted on a hangar roof which said CALIFORNIA THIS WAY. Underneath the sign was an arrow pointing in the direction the balloon was going.

"Thanks for the information," I yelled, just kidding around with my words and hoping the sign wasn't painted backwards.

The first airport I flew over in Ohio had a big YOU'RE WELCOME sign painted on one of its hangar roofs.

"That's real polite of you," I yelled to the sign.

THAT'S THE WAY IT GETS FARTHER OUT WEST YOU FLY a sign on a hangar roof at the next airport said.

So I was heading west after all. Buoyed up by this news, I sat down on the floor and started typing this letter.

Then I heard what sounded like a police-car siren, I looked at

the highway below for the police car chasing a speeding vehicle. But the siren was coming from a much smaller balloon than mine that was chasing me and catching up.

BALLOON PATROL it said on the balloon and in its gondola were two policemen. Their balloon got nearer. Over one of those hand-held bullhorns, a policeman told me "Full rover do her hide end stop."

"What? I didn't make that out."

He shut the siren off and said "I told you to pull over to the side and stop."

"I don't know how."

"Just step on the brakes."

"There are no brakes."

He threw a pair of brakes into my gondola, I told him I was no auto mechanic and didn't know how to install them.

"Instead," I said, "throw over a hook to catch onto my gondola and you can bring me down or fly me back that way."

"By hook or by crook this bum's going to try and get away with that kid's balloon," he said to his partner through the bullhorn.

His partner grabbed the bullhorn from him and said into it "What should we do, Ike? Call in more patrols to block his way ahead?"

Ike grabbed back the bullhorn and said into it "And let those other Charlies get credit for collaring him? No sir. You want to see what we're going to do, watch me."

Ike drew his revolver and shot at my balloon. The balloon didn't go pop as I thought it would. Instead it started to deflate over Indiana, descend over Illinois, and when the last of its air sissed out over Iowa, it landed and flopped over on the ground, the flattened balloon covering me like a giant banana peel.

The police landed their balloon in the same meadow. Ike put handcuffs on my wrists and was about to bring down his club on my skull.

"I don't think we have jurisdiction on the ground," his partner said.

"Ahhh, you're such a stickler for the law," Ike said. He removed the cuffs and said to me "You're lucky this time, sport. But let me catch you in the air with that kid's balloon again or any kid's balloon, no matter how large or small, and you'll really be in a hole."

I finished this letter before they took off, and asked them to mail it. I thought it might be a while before I found a mailbox, while they could drop it in one when they got back to their Central Park precinct in New York. I still hope to see you, Kev, and always my best.

Rudy

Dear Kevin:

Where did I leave off in my last letter? Oh yeah. In that huge Iowa meadow, with no houses or roads around for miles and the police balloon rising above my head.

"Good riddance," I whispered to myself, glad to see them go. But Ike said through the bullhorn from a hundred feet up: "What's that you said, sport?"

"Good afternoon, officers, is what I said. And have a very pleasant journey back to New York."

"We've got ourselves a real wise guy down there," Ike said to his partner through the bullhorn, and they sailed back to the ground.

I was already set for a nap, typewriter case under my head as a pillow and some writing paper under and on top of me as sheets. I jumped up and ran in the direction where the sun was setting, which I knew was west and where California must lie about 1,500 miles from here. The balloon landed and the policemen climbed out and chased me.

I saw a horse grazing in a field, but no ordinary horse. This one only had three legs. The front leg was in the middle of its body instead of at one of its sides. Sort of like the front wheel of a tricycle, with the two rear wheels where they should normally be. But if the front leg was on either of its two sides, this horse would have toppled over, instead of staying perfectly balanced as it did. So maybe this is the way a horse should normally have its legs, and all those other horses with four legs on their sides are the ones that aren't built right.

I leaped on the horse's back and said "Giddy-up." The horse didn't move. Maybe out West they say "Giddy-yup," so I said "Giddy-yup" to the horse. And then "Giddy-yap" and "Giddy-ap" and "Giddy-ep" and "Giddy-ip," but none of these commands worked either.

The policemen were about fifty feet from me now. I had to get a move on quick, so I said "Come on, horse, let's get a move on. Then a move in. A move an? Move un? Just a move? A moo? A mov? A mo?"

That struck home. The horse lifted its head and looked at me.

"Mo?" I said.

"Neigh," the horse said.

"Not Mo?"

"Neigh neigh."

"Then just plain Mo? Is that your name?"

"Yeigh yeigh."

"Well, let's get a move on, Just Plain Mo."

He stretched his neck to get at some fresh grass. He had that kind of sickly look that people get when they eat something that doesn't agree with them, which I can understand would happen with people when they eat grass. But I didn't want to be kicking his sour belly and making him more upset and then angry with me. Finally he burped, said "Ahhh," as if that was all he needed, and started running as fast as a racehorse and without any coaxing from me. Only he was running backwards to New York, which was the opposite direction I wanted to go, but at the right speed.

He galloped backwards past the policemen and rode this way for ten minutes, when he stopped at a stream to drink.

"Great ride," I said. "Now if you can just turn around and face your rear end to the west and your front to the east and run the same way, I might be able to get some place on you."

He wouldn't turn, so I got off and pushed him around to where his rear faced west and where he could now run backwards all he liked. I got back on and said "Okay, Just Plain Mo, up-giddy. Then yup-giddy. Then ap-giddy. Ep-giddy? Ip-giddy?"

Sour belly or not, I wasn't waiting for those police to catch up with me, so I gave Just Plain Mo a kick. He started to run. Only now he ran in the direction where his head pointed: the right way for a horse to run and at the same racehorse speed, but still towards New York.

"Whoa, Just Plain Mo," I said. But he galloped forwards for another ten minutes and then stopped at a stream to cool his legs and drink.

I got off and turned him around to face west again and pointed.

"See where I'm pointing? There's a boy out there I want to see badly, so that's the direction I want you to go. Now you can have your choice of which way you want to run. You want to go frontwards, then do so all you want. Or you want to run backwards, then I'll turn your rear around so it faces California, and you can run that way for as long as you want. But whether you run rearwards or headwards it's got to be westwards, understandwards?"

I got back on him and said "Okay, Just Plain Mo. Giddy-up or up-giddy, but get your giggy going, you hear?"

He galloped backwards to the east for a few minutes, then stopped in a field to munch grass.

I knew I'd never get him to go west no matter which way I pointed him. And I didn't want to go farther east on him, and what other two main directions are there but north and south. So I decided to point his head north or south and let him run whichever way he wanted—backwards or forwards, I didn't much care. When he felt like stopping, since I could never get him to stop,

I'd look for a different type horse that runs where you tell it to and always forward. Or if I could find one, a three-legged horse who only runs west.

I pulled Just Plain Mo around to where his head faced north. And he pulled his rear around to where it pointed south. Then I climbed up on him and said "
G
i
d
d
y
,
u
p
" But he wouldn't move. So I said "
P
u
,
y
d
d
i
g
.
" But he still wouldn't move. I thought maybe I'd been too rough on him with my kicking and harsh words, and what he'd like more is some neck-petting and a song. So I sang very softly into his ear as I petted him:

"I know a little filly in Kalamazoo

"who rides a spotted missy I'll introduce you to.

"This missy's got three legs also

"and a fourth for class
"and her own grazing ground
"with the greenest-tasting grass.
"And a stream that runs like water
"and a yellow mane and scarlet bow
"and she's hankering for a mixed-up stallion
"so get a move on, Just Plain Mo."

He trotted off sideways, but still to the east. When he got himself up to a gallop, he was able to run as fast sideways as he was forwards and back. After his usual five-to-ten-minute run, he stopped for water and grass and then lay down to sleep.

What I'll do when he wakes up, I thought, is get on him and stay with him while he runs whichever way he wants: backwards, forwards or sideways, but always east. Past Indiana and Ohio and all the other states I ballooned over, till he reaches New York. Then across the Atlantic and Europe and Russia and China and the Pacific Ocean till he reaches California, where I'll get off and let him complete his round-the-world trip by himself.

But that would take so long that you'd probably have moved so many times by then that I'd never know where to find you. Instead,

I typed this letter. When I'm done with it, I'll tie it around Just Plain Mo's neck. On the letter's envelope I've already written "To whom it may concern. If you see this horse running past a mailbox or eating, drinking or sleeping by one, please creep up on him, remove this envelope and drop it in the mailbox. Thanks loads."

Well, I still hope to see you one day, Kev, though don't go betting your coin collection on my reaching California soon.

Rudy

Dear Kevin:

The next thing I'm going to write about might seem unbelievable to you. Maybe it never did happen and only took place in my dreams. But I've got the bruises from falling to prove it happened. Though maybe these bruises won't be there when I wake up, if I'm also only writing this letter in my dreams.

No, I'm positive what happened to me really did. But let me write about it before I forget it. Because if I write about it after I forget it, there won't be anything to write about.

If I don't write this letter and we later really meet and you tell me you received it, it would probably mean you got this letter in your dreams. If you actually show me this letter and swear you didn't write it, it could mean that someone else dreamed up what happened to me and sent you a letter about it and signed my name. One way or the other, you'd at least have received a letter telling what happened to me. Which would be a lot more than you'd receive from me if I forgot everything I wanted to write you because I took too long discussing whether it happened in or out of my dreams.

First off, after writing you that last letter about Just Plain Mo, I fell asleep with my head resting on his belly and woke up in a cave. Some light came in through a small slit in the ceiling. All I could see through the slit was sky. I wondered how I got in the cave, as it was sealed. Just Plain Mo? He would have had to put me on his back and carry me in here while I was asleep, and I don't remember that.

I looked around for a way out of the cave and found nothing.

Not even a hole big enough for the mouse I heard scurrying around. One answer how I got here was that I sleepwalked in. Then, still sleepwalking, or sleepsealing, I sealed the cave's opening I'd come through and woke up. As for the mouse, if it didn't come in with me, I suppose it just sleepscurried in here and then sealed up its own little hole.

The only way out then might be to fall asleep and sleepwalk to where I sealed the cave. Then I could push away the stone or whatever it was I used to seal the opening, and still sleepwalking, slip out of the cave and wake up.

So I fell asleep. When I awoke I was in a room with a table and chair. A plate of steaming spaghetti was on the table with a jar of grated cheese. There was no silverware. A lit candle was on the floor and the mouse seemed to be gone.

I checked the room for windows and doors. It had none. Just four walls and a ceiling and floor. There were no holes anywhere for a light fixture or electrical plug, nor any trapdoors or secret exits that I could find. Once more, I didn't know how I got in here. Maybe after I fell asleep to sleepwalk, I sleepwalked out of the cave into this room and then sealed the entrance to the room and woke up. As for the mouse, I suppose if it didn't follow me and wasn't hiding in here, that it just stayed in the cave or sleepscurried to the outdoors or some other cave or room.

But where'd the food and candle come from? Maybe there was a kitchen between the cave and room. And during my sleepwalking I stopped to sleepcook a pot of spaghetti, sleeplight a candle and then sleepbring the food and candle and maybe even the table and chair into this room. The reason there was no silverware could be that when I'm by myself I prefer eating with my hands.

It was a good thing I sleepcooked some food, as I was very hungry. I ate, and then feeling drowsy from so much food, shut my eyes and felt myself falling asleep.

Great, I thought. Because if I sleepwalked in here, maybe I'll sleepwalk out to the place where I first fell asleep beside Just Plain Mo. In fact, maybe I'm such a good sleepwalker, seeing how I cooked a dinner while asleep, that I'll be able to sleepwalk not only out of this room but all the way to Palo Alto.

I went to sleep. When I woke up I was in a huge banquet hall. A long table for about fifty people was in the middle of the hall with many lit candles in a candelabra on it. A plate of food, shiny silverware, cloth napkin and bottle of champagne and champagne glass were in front of the one setting at the far end of the table. Again, I couldn't find any windows, doors or openings of any kind.

I see what it is, I thought. I'm still outside next to Just Plain Mo and dreaming. Well, I'm tired of going from room to room in my dreams. But I'll still have some food and wine before I wake myself up. Because if this is a dream I'm in, then I must have come a long ways in it from that last room to this banquet hall to be so hungry again.

I stuffed myself with steak and potatoes. With the champagne, I toasted to my good health and successful trip to Palo Alto. Then I bowed and bid adieu to all the empty places at the table and pinched my cheeks real hard. But I wasn't able to wake myself up.

Finally I yelled "Hey, anybody around?" I didn't know why I didn't yell this before. Maybe I thought nobody was around to hear me. "Come on, if anybody's around. Let me know you're here by showing yourself or just tapping on the walls or hidden ceiling or door. Even if this might only be a dream I'm in, or even a dream that I'm dreaming I'm in, I still always like to know who else is in them."

No answer, taps or anything.

So far, the only way I've been able to get out of these rooms or the cave was to go to sleep. But this time when I sleepwalk, I won't stop off at the kitchen to cook a meal. Because it might be that after I cook these great dinners, I always look for another room with a table and chair to eat them in. I'll just sleepwalk straight to the outside, wake up, and find my food out there.

I drank some more champagne and fell asleep. This time I woke up in a room as big and empty as a Major League indoor stadium if all the stands, stairs and fences had been removed. I was the only person or thing in this room except for a light bulb that hung on a wire halfway down from the middle of the ceiling. The floor was made of marble, the walls of white plaster, and the ceiling, from

what I could make out as it was that high up, of carved wood. It took me several hours to inspect the room for doors or openings. There were none, not even a crack in the wall or floor. It was as if the marble had been put in and walls painted the day before, and had only now dried.

Maybe if I fell asleep again I'd be able to sleepwalk out of this room and past the banquet hall to the room with the ordinary-sized table with no silverware on it. Then I'd stand on the table in that room and try and break through the ceiling and climb out to what might be the free sky above. So I curled up in a corner, still a bit groggy from all the champagne I drank in that last banquet hall, and fell asleep.

I woke in a room that was as long as two aircraft carriers and so wide and high that it could have fitted three Major League stadiums in it and on top of the stadiums, a cathedral with tall spires. In the middle of the room was something like an enormous stage. It took me three minutes just to run to it. It was a round table, big enough to fit the three baseball teams around and all the families, relatives and friends of the players and maybe a couple thousand of their fans and all the groundskeepers and peanut and

soda vendors too. The light in the room came from somewhere way above me. But it was so far up that I couldn't tell whether it was a ceiling or windows the light was coming through or just an opened roof.

There was one setting and stool at the table. And the food, on a soggy paper plate, was two cold hot dogs and splash of ketchup and pint container of milk with a chewed straw inside.

Now it didn't seem possible that I had sleepwalked into this room. Because why would I cook two hot dogs in wherever the kitchen was, leave them with the milk in the middle of this room, and then go to one end of the room about a half mile away from the table to wake up? Only to come back to the hot dogs, which by then would be cold and wrinkled, and the milk, which if I got it cold, was now warm.

No, someone must have brought me and my typewriter here when I was asleep, and had the table set up for me before I woke up. But who?

"Hey?" I yelled. "What's the idea of all this? First off, if you know anything about me, then you know I don't like hot dogs—wrinkled or smooth. And if I must eat them because there's no other food around, at least give me mustard with them instead of ketchup. Also chocolate syrup for the milk, if you don't mind. I'm thirsty and the milk with the syrup mixed in it is the only way I can ever get it down."

No voice answered except my echo, which said "There's no mustard or syrup around, so take what you got or starve."

I ate the hot dogs and milk, as the next rooms I sleepwalked through might be very far away and the food in them even worse. Then I stretched out on the table to fall asleep. Even if there were doors or openings here, the room was so big that it would take days to find them. Since there wasn't any more food around, where would I get the energy for such a long search? I'll just wait till I awake in a much smaller room before I start looking for an opening to the outside.

I woke up in the same room. The furniture and milk container were gone and I was lying on the floor. Did I sleepwalk through a hidden opening that I can only find when I'm sleepwalking, and carry the table out with me and then return to the middle of this room to wake up? Impossible. Even if there was a door large enough to get that table through, and another room large enough to store it, the table would still have been too heavy to carry alone. I would have needed the help of all those fans, players and groundskeepers. Or maybe while I was asleep I broke the table up into a million or more pieces and carried it out of the room that way, pile by pile. Anyway, either from lack of sleep or carrying all those piles out of the room, I was much too tired to look for the opening I might have carried the wood through, and fell asleep.

The place I woke up in this time was absolutely black. It could have been the same room as before, or one of the other rooms I've been in since I fell asleep next to Just Plain Mo. What could I do but bump around or go to sleep again till either daylight came or someone uncovered the cave slit or relit the candle in the first room or one of the many candles in the banquet hall or replaced the light bulb in that next room as big as a stadium or turned on the light switch or let up the window shade or opened the roof again in that last and largest of the rooms.

I woke in the dark again and walked with my free hand and typewriter waving before me. I actually hoped to bump into something, which might tell me where I was. But nothing got in my way or I didn't get in the way of anything moving past me. Then I ran in what I hoped was one direction. I decided that if this was still a dream I was in, I'd crash into a wall and wake up.

I ran for about fifteen minutes and didn't crash into anything. So maybe I was in an even larger room than the one where three indoor stadiums, two aircraft carriers and a cathedral with tall spires on it could have stood on top of one another or side by side with all those fans.

"Hey," I yelled, "is this some kind of joke? Well, I'll tell you it isn't some kind of joke. It's no joke at all. That's right. Because I'm not laughing. And I don't hear anyone else laughing. Maybe if I heard someone laughing I might consider it a joke. Or if I started laughing you might start laughing, and then we could both consider it a joke. If you really want to get me laughing so you can start laughing, turn on the lights. Or show me the door or get me outside or sing the Happy Birthday ditty or something, but I've had enough, you hear?"

Nothing answered me but my echo a minute later, which sang a song in another language and then applauded when it was over.

Maybe if I had talked faster, my echo would have come back to me sooner. But I still hadn't a clue how far away I was from the wall.

I fell asleep. What else could I do? And now this is the strangest part. When I awoke I was in midair somewhere being carried along in the dark. Certainly an outdoor wind or indoor breeze was flying through my hair and clothes. And I felt I would have been blown off whatever this long thing I was on if I didn't hold on tight.

It wasn't the neck or back of a bird I was on, for I heard a clump-clumping of feet from below and no flapping of wings. And I wasn't being held by anything—just lying on some kind of cloth. Below the cloth it felt like the warm part of a body, like tightened muscle or bone. I couldn't tell exactly what part of the body it was, as I couldn't find a hole in the cloth and the cloth was too strong to tear.

To test how high up I was, I got the door knocker out of the typewriter case and dropped it off the side. I never heard it reach bottom. That doesn't mean it didn't. Because there could have been a thick carpet below or water or sand or mud. But if it was one of those soft things below, then the walking sound I heard before would have been a squash-squashing or slosh-sloshing instead of that clump-clumping. So I must have been very high up and the sound of the door knocker hitting the ground was just too far away to hear.

I crawled farther along this thing to find out more about it. When I reached my arm above and partly around it while holding onto the cloth with my other hand, all I could feel was air. It was like crawling in the dark on a narrow plank between two moving buildings many floors up.

The closest it came to any body part now was a finger. Not just because of its cigar shape. But because when I was crawling, I fell into a ditch of about ten feet deep. That could have been the crack where one finger joint joins the other. One finger I knew it couldn't be was the thumb. For a thumb only has two joints and one crack between them. And I would have fallen off the thumb's second joint by now, since I was already on the third.

Another thing it couldn't be was a cigar. Though it was round, long and warm like one that was newly lit, I didn't know of a cigar that had finger joints on it. What did scare me for a moment was maybe this was a very unusual cigar with joints and cracks. If it was one like that and lit, maybe I was crawling to its burning ash. But then I knew I'd feel the heat of the ash long before I reached it.

So I decided it was a finger I was on. And the tight cloth around it was part of a glove, as maybe its hand gets cold or the thing whose hand it is likes fancy clothes or plays golf or was out gardening. Of course, this hand could be like none I'd ever known. With more joints and cracks than the usual type fingers. And with the rough cloth being the hand's skin—smooth to someone its own size, but rough to me because I can feel every pore and finger groove.

Not to take chances with whatever kind of hand it was, I stopped crawling. Since if I was crawling along the finger to the wrist part, it might be unsafe if let's say the palm was cupped into a deep ditch I could fall in. Or if I was crawling to the finger tip, then the next ditch I came to might be a drop of several hundred feet with no carpet below.

"Excuse me, whoever you are," I yelled. "If you are a you. Or whatever you are. But where are you taking me, if I can ask? If I can't ask, please don't think anything more of it as I won't ask again. But if you don't mind my asking, maybe I could also ask if you're taking me some place you think I might not want to go to. Or maybe I've hooked onto you by accident and you didn't know I was here till I just mentioned it and you definitely don't want me along. If you didn't know I was here, then please forget I told you. But maybe it's best for me you do know I'm here and also something about me. For you see, I'm quite the harmless little fellow, so don't think you have to flick me off like you would a flea. I can get off myself nice and peaceful-like anytime you want me to, though I think it would be best if you first stopped. If you did know I was here and in fact stuck me on you, then all I ask is you try not to trip or run into any wall or chair or anyone the same size as you who might be in your way. And maybe you could also give me a brief warning if you suddenly feel like leaping through the air. By the way, if this is your finger I'm on and I'm yelling too low for you to hear me from way out wherever your ears or hearing organs are, please say so and I'll yell extra loud."

No answer. So I told myself: "Relax. Act like this is a roller coaster you're on. You know: enjoy the ride, get a little scared, even scream your lungs out if you want, but don't stand up or let go."

I held on tight till this thing stopped moving. Then something soft and about the size and shape of a double mattress standing on its end nudged me off the finger to the ground. I quickly stuck my fingers in my ears, as I knew I was so close to this thing's feet now that its clump-clumping might sound like bombs going off near my head.

Even with my ears plugged, my eardrums must have gotten a bit shattered. The noise wasn't any big feet clumping away either. But what sounded like one whale of a door being screeched shut and then this slam as loud as that cathedral and two aircraft carriers and three indoor stadiums with all its ticket booths and vending machines and cases of empty soda bottles collapsing around me at the same time. And no matter how loud it was to me, there is a possibility that this thing, maybe realizing how small my ears are and how much sound they can take, might even have had the consideration to close the door as gently and quietly as it could.

But I was outdoors again and was going to stay awake till morning and I could see the place I'd just been released from.

When daylight came I found myself at the bottom of a mountain. It was half a mile high and flat right up to its top like a modern skyscraper, but with no windows or doors on it, just rock. It was a mystery to me. How come I was now at the bottom of this thing when yesterday or sometime before I was in a flat field with Just Plain Mo snoring away beside me and no mountain or even a hill or tree in sight?

"Hey, you in there," I yelled, banging on the side of the mountain as if it was a door. "That's right—I'm talking to you, because I want some things cleared up. I don't like mystery stories, understand? If I have to read one because there are no other books around, then I like the endings neatly tied up. First tell me whose rooms were they in there? And who brought me into your mountain and then moved me from cave to room to banquet hall? Is there a kitchen inside? Many kitchens connecting up all those rooms? Or just a couple of short-order cafes and a classy restaurant that also has take-out orders? If not, then who cooked all that food? At least give me the recipe for the spaghetti sauce I had in the first room or tell me how you knew I liked my steak medium-rare. And who lit the candles or kept blowing them out or unscrewed the light bulbs or carried me past the door in this mountain on his or her finger and nudged me to the ground? I'm sitting here till all my questions are answered, you got that straight?"

I stayed by this mountainside for two days and nights. I thought that if whoever or whatever it was inside didn't want to show itself in the day, maybe it would whisper the answers into my ear at night when it couldn't be seen.

It never came out. Oh, maybe if I had stayed there for a month or year or even near to the end of what could be a long lifetime—maybe then, when I was old and bent, it would come out and explain why this and that happened or just hand me a note with all the answers on it or just one answer for them all and then clump back inside.

Because it's possible that creatures like that thing with the big finger live on for centuries if not eons, and so have lots of time to spare and can deal with matters whenever they like and without feeling the years are flitting past and nothing's getting done. While I didn't want to spend most of my life waiting for this thing to take a week to finish picking its teeth after a twenty-year-long snack or something, before it got up to answer my knocking at the mountainside. For I still wanted to see you before you graduated grade school and got married and became a great-grandfather, and also to do a few more things with my own life too.

So I walked away from the mountain. Headed in the direction where I saw smoke from a few miles off. Maybe there was a person there who could give me some answers about that mountain. I also sat down at a cool spot to write this letter, which I'll mail to you first chance I get.

All my best,
Rudy

Dear Kevin:

It took half a day to reach the place where the smoke was coming from. It was a small cabin in about a quarter-acre clearing in the woods. There were no fences, paths, garden, graves, pets, cars, bikes, wash, trash cans or antennae or really any sign of life other than this simple cabin with its one window beside the front door and smoke curling out of its chimney.

I knocked on the door. Nobody answered. I knocked much harder. Still no one answered or came to the door. Now where there's continuous smoke from a chimney there's usually someone tending a fire. Unless the cabin was burning away slowly from the inside or the wood was throwing itself into the fire.

So I pounded and kicked the door. Someone pounded and kicked back. I knocked twice and someone knocked back twice. I tapped three short taps and a long one, and the person inside did the same.

"Anybody in?" I said.

"Anybody in?" a voice said, neither male nor female, just scratchy and maybe old.

"Then someone must be in," I said.

"Then someone must be in," the voice said.

"All kidding aside," I said—

"All kidding aside," the voice said—

"No, I mean really, all kidding aside. For you see—"

"No, I mean really, all kidding aside. For you see—"

"I could use a hot meal and a night's sleep in a real bed."

"I could use a night's meal and a real sleep in a hot bed."

"Who's mimicking me?" I said.

"Who's mimicking me?" the voice said.

"Nobody's mimicking you. You're mimicking me. And you're doing a pretty bad job of it with that 'night's meal and a real sleep in a hot bed.'"

"Nobody's mimicking you. You're mimicking me. And you're doing a night's job of it with that 'real meal and a hot sleep in a pretty bad bed.'"

"Okay. Who is this *me* I'm speaking to then?"

"Okay. Who is this *me* I'm speaking to then?"

"A man."

"A man."

"Well, listen here, man, you opening this door or not?"

"Well, listen here, man, you opening this door or not?"

"You want me to open the door, I will."

"You want me to open the door, I will."

I waited for him to open the door. He didn't. I tried the doorknob. The door was locked. Then the man tried the doorknob. The door didn't move.

"Can't you get out?" I said.

"Can't you get out?" he said.

"How can you say 'Can't you get out?' when I'm outside?"

"How can you say 'Can't you get out?' when I'm outside?"

"You can't be outside if you're inside behind the door."

"You can't be outside if you're inside behind the door."

"We'll see."

"We'll see."

I leaned my typewriter against the door and the case against the window, so if the door or window opened I'd hear the typewriter or case fall. Then I ran around the cabin. The only door and window were in front. Both were locked, with the typewriter and case still up against them, so the man couldn't have gone out

to see if I was the one who was outside. The window shade was down. I couldn't see in the cabin. Smoke was still curling out of the chimney.

"I just ran around the cabin and proved to myself that I'm the one who's outside," I said.

"I just ran around the cabin and proved to myself—"

"But you couldn't have."

"But you couldn't have."

"Look. If you're locked in there or afraid to come out, tell me and I'll help you."

"Look. If you're locked in there—"

"All right," I said. "I know what you're going to say."

"All right," he said. "I know—"

"I said all right, all right, I know."

"I said all right, all right, I know."

"Have you anything else to say?"

"Have you anything else to say?"

"Nothing."

"Nothing."

"Then goodbye."

"Then goodbye."

I walked into the woods, sorry I wouldn't have a hot meal and place to sleep tonight and some answers about that mountain. Then I ran back and kicked the cabin door and said "There, I just proved who's outside. Because I just walked into the woods, heading west, following the sun, feet on the earth and mud in my shoes as I moved, brushing away shrubs, pausing to sip from a brook, pick a berry off a bush, a root out of the ground, trail the tracks of a deer, things you could never do as long as you stay in the cabin."

"Oh yeah?"

"Ah," I said.

"Oh," he said.

"Something wrong?"

He kicked the door. "Just a little bellyache, but I'll be okay."

"Sure you won't need a doctor?"

"Sure you won't need a doctor?"

"Why? I wasn't the one who complained of an ache."

"Why? I wasn't the one—"

"Forget it. You did, and my arguing is useless, so I'll really have to be leaving for good now. See ya."

"Forget it. You did, and my arguing is useless, so I'll really have to be leaving for good now. See ya."

"Fine. Where you leaving to—somewhere else in the cabin?" and I laughed.

"Fine," he said laughing. "Where you leaving to—somewhere else in the cabin?"

"I didn't start laughing till I finished my sentence."

"I didn't start laughing till I finished my sentence."

"That's a lie."

"That's a lie."

"And it wasn't your sentence originally but mine."

"And it wasn't your sentence originally but mine."

"Just as that last sentence was."

"Just as that last sentence was."

"Anything you say."

"Anything you say."

"Ditto."

"Ditto."

"And ditto your ditto."

"And ditto your ditto."

"It's obvious you'll never make any sense to me, so goodbye."

"It's obvious you'll never make any sense to me, so goodbye."

"Okay—goodbye. Now where you going?"

"Okay—goodbye. Now where you going?"

"Well, I'm going through the woods again. Where are you?"

"I'm going through the woods again. Where are you?"

"You left out the 'well.'"

"Well?"

"Well, I'm waiting for you to go through the woods again."

"Well, I'm waiting for you to go through the woods again."

"I am," and I did.

"I am" were the last words I heard him say.

I went through the woods. I would have left that last letter and now this one on his doorstep, but I didn't think the postman came by his cabin anymore. Since if this man ever did write a letter, I'm sure it would be an exact copy of a letter someone had sent him, including the sender's name and address for his and the same date the sender had put on top. That wouldn't make for a very interesting correspondence for the person writing him, so my guess is that people have given up sending him letters and he now has nothing to copy and mail.

Though from you I wouldn't mind getting a copy of this letter, I love getting mail and so far haven't received a letter from you. It would also mean you got at least one of my letters and know I'm trying to get to Palo Alto. But since I don't know where I'll be in the next few days unless I get to Palo Alto by then, maybe you better hold off copying this letter and mailing it till I arrive.

Very best, Rudy

Dear Kevin:

Soon after writing the last letter I thought that the one thing I haven't run into yet in my travels west are pixies, when sure enough two of them were standing in my way. Now I don't believe in pixies or fairies or any sprites or mythical beings like that, so I scooted around them as if they weren't there. But one of them crouched behind me and the other pushed me over his fellow pixie's back.

"Oops. Must've stumbled over a stone," I said, getting up. "Rockier terrain than I first thought. Got to be extra careful where I walk," and I continued on, still convinced pixies didn't exist. Especially pixies like these two, with their large pointy ears and hairless square skulls and flopping feet as long and lean as their bodies were tall and thin. And a nose that was curled up like a watch spring, and every time one of them sneezed, the other's nose spun out like a New Year's Eve noisemaker and whistled as it unwound.

Suddenly the first pixie tackled me to the ground from behind, and the second one ran back and forth over my body with his feet flattening my face.

I pushed it off, got up and straightened my nose.

"Must've been bowled over by a savage bull buffalo," I said. "Then had the whole herd stampede over me, forget where they were stampeding to, and turn around and stampede back. Rougher territory than I expected, the West. Primitive and untamed."

"Hello. I'm Pete, she's Pat, and we're pixies," one of them said.

"No. I'm Pete, she's Pat, and we're pixies," the second one said.

"Oh. We're both Petes, we're both Pats, and we're both pixies," they said, kicking me in the pants and sending me sprawling to the ground.

I cupped my hand behind my ear and said "What's that I hear but the late summer sounds of chittering crickets in the fields.

And do I not also feel the strong western winter winds blowing hard at my rear?"

They helped me up, with their scarves swatted the clods of dirt off my clothes, then each began polishing one of my suede shoes. They continued polishing up the front of my body and down the back of it, giving special attention to my elbows, knuckles and knees. Then while one was putting a shine on my typewriter case trim, the other stuck a twig between my shoe and lit it.

I stamped around from the flame in my shoe and thought I must have stepped on some dried leaves which this much stronger wind out West had ignited and that much stronger western wind had fanned into a fire. That was the only way I could explain how the fire started, as I plunged my burning foot into a pond.

"Wouldn't you think he'd want to take his shoe off first before he put his foot in the pond?" the one called Pete or Pat said.

"You mean wouldn't you think he'd want to take his foot off first before he put his shoe in the pond?" the other called Pete or Pat said.

They dragged me out of the pond. Then each grabbed one of my feet and tugged at it as if to pull off my foot with the shoe. I kicked them away and tried standing on only the foot that hadn't been burned.

"It's wilder out West than anyone could have imagined," I said, falling over. "With the fish in the ponds more ferocious than the buffalo, and about as large."

I got my typewriter and limped away. The two of them got on either side of me and limped along.

"You think he's thinking he doesn't think we're real?" one said.

"I think he's thinking if he thought out loud we were real, he'd think inside he wasn't," the other said.

"What do you think of what we think you're now thinking?" both said.

I took off my shoe and sock, emptied the watery shoe and squeezed the soaked sock over him or her. Then I removed the scarf from around his or her neck, wrapped my burnt foot in it and put my sock and shoe on.

"That's my brand new scarf," he or she said.

"Made special for us by elves in the woods," the other said.

"There are no such things as elves," the first one said. And to me: "Aren't you even going to say why you stole my scarf?"

"Maybe the cat's got his tongue," the second one said.

"Then all we have to do is catch the cat to get his tongue back and he can tell us why he stole my scarf."

"Here kitty, kitty," they both said, humped over and circling me in opposite directions. They bumped heads and fell down, where each grabbed one of my legs and dumped me on the ground next to them. Then one sat on my knees, removed my shoes and socks, put the scarf back on its neck and my shoes and socks back on my feet, but with the shoes on first and the socks over them. "While at the same time the second one sat on my chest and tickled my neck till my mouth stayed open and then caught hold of my tongue.

"Here's the thieving cat," this one said, pinching my tongue.

"Yyybbb mmnnn llwww," I said.

"Must mean 'meow' in whatever land it comes from," one of them said, still holding my tongue.

"And 'meow' could mean 'I'm sorry for stealing your scarf, kind lady or sir,' in whatever land it comes from, so give back his tongue."

They got off me and stood up.

"Birds out West are even more vicious than the fish and buffalo," I said. "Fly right by your face, pitch you over with their wings and think your tongue is a worm in the ground for them to pull out. I'll be glad when I find my way out of these wild woods."

"Why didn't you say so?" they said. "Go between those two vines and down a winding path and you'll find a stream and docked canoe."

Now I knew that they knew that I knew that what they said was an out-and-out lie. And what they really wanted me to do was take the opposite direction from the one they told me to go. To avoid whatever trap they had waiting for me in that opposite direction, I took the opposite direction of the opposite direction they wanted me to go, sure that that was where the stream and canoe were.

While walking in the direction they never expected me to go, my foot got caught in the noose of a snare and I was hurled into the air and wound up being hung upside down by a rope attached to a branch. From way up there I could see the stream and canoe, which were in the opposite direction of the opposite direction I thought they would be.

"Hey," I said, "I really like it up here, hanging upside down. With the noose biting my ankle and cutting my skin. And the blood rushing to my head and giving me a fantastic nosebleed and about to knock me out cold and maybe finish me for good."

I said this so they would believe the opposite of the opposite of what I said and think I did like it up there and then cut me loose and hoist me down.

But one of them said "If he really likes it up there so much, I think we should cut him loose and bring him down, don't you?"

"I absolutely do," the other said, and they ran into the woods.

Instead of doing all the things I would normally do to try and get free, such as bouncing up and down to break the branch. Or swinging back and forth to catch hold of another branch. Or flipping myself up to grab the rope and untie the noose. I did the opposite of all those, which was nothing, and in an hour the branch had drooped to the ground from my weight and I undid the noose and crawled away.

I got my typewriter out of the pond they had sunk it in. While the typewriter was drying in the sun, I untangled the typewriter ribbon they had strung across the treetops, and rolled it back on its spool. Then I screwed the typewriter case handle back on, located my papers, envelopes and stamps in the nests of attacking hornets and snakes they had put them in, and walked between those vines and down a winding path to the stream and got in the canoe. As the current carried me downstream, I began and am now finishing this letter about the two pixies I met who didn't exist.

Your friend,
Rudy

Dear Kevin:

I awoke in the canoe when the stream was widening into a river and paddled with my hands to the first landing I could find with a mailbox on it. It was a small dock and a man and boy were fishing from it.

"Excuse me," I said, mailing my letters, "but what state we in?"

"Have no idea," the man said. "I don't hail from around here."

"Where you from?"

"About five miles upstream where two pixies once gave me a canoe."

"There are no such things as pixies," I said.

"I know. But I took the canoe from the place they pointed to and landed at this dock. Then like they asked me to, I sent the canoe back upstream."

"Nobody told me to send my canoe back upstream."

"Send your canoe back upstream," a voice, something like Pat or Pete's through a loudspeaker, said from somewhere way out in the woods.

"You hear anything?" I said.

"You mean something like a pixie's voice over a loudspeaker saying you should send your canoe back upstream?" the man said.

"Yes."

"No, I didn't hear anything."

"Neither did I." I turned the canoe around and gave it a shove. We watched it drift upriver against the current and disappear around the bend I'd just come from.

"You know," I said, "your travels sound a little like mine. "Where were you before you happened to stumble upon that canoe?"

"Before the canoe," the man said, "I came across a lonely cabin in the woods. The man inside kept insisting he had to be outside if I was inside the cabin, so I walked away leaving him thinking he was walking away from a real extreme hermit who hadn't left his home since the day he was born and had no intention to. Now before the hermit, I was either in a mountain or I wasn't. All I know is I gained twenty pounds from all the chow and swill I had in the rooms and banquet halls inside this mountain that I only might have dreamt I was in. Before the mountain, I know it was no dream that I escaped from a balloon patrol on the back of a three-legged horse I found in a field."

"Not a black and brown stallion who'd only ride eastwards," I said.

"That's the direction."

"And who'd only answer to the name Just Plain Mo?"

"That's what he was called."

"Then it couldn't have been the same horse."

"Wouldn't think so," he said. "Too much of a coincidence.

Now as to where I was before I met Just Plain Mo is so long ago for a man my age that I plumb forgot. All I know is I ended up at a place I always wanted to be since I was this boy's age. And that's sitting on a dock with a mailbox on it, by a river with all the fish I'd ever want to catch in my life."

"Really biting, eh?"

"Haven't caught one since I first canoed down here, but the boy got one this winter."

"The winter before that," the boy said. "Had to dig a hole through the ice to get it though."

"Not a hole in the river," the man said, "but one he dug in the road up beyond. And there it was. Wrapped in newspaper with a string tied around it, just ready to be pulled out. A real whopper."

"As big as this," the boy said. He brought his hands together till the fingers joined.

"Aren't you exaggerating a little?" the man said.

"Maybe by a little. But we're still eating it, aren't we? And that was fourteen months ago the fish was caught."

"Half of it we smoked."

"You smoked it. Because you said it was too dangerous to my health if I even smoked a bit of it."

"And it wouldn't be? Start this young one on bad habits like that and he'll be drinking my whiskey next."

"You don't have any whiskey," the boy said.

"There, you see? He must have stolen it right from under my nose. Probably getting soused when I'm out here all day fishing. I knew you'd come to no good."

"You never had any whiskey," the boy said. "All we ever had to drink besides river water was twenty-four cases of frozen grape juice that floated downstream one day and which in one sitting you drank all by yourself straight."

"I wouldn't have drunk the juice straight if you hadn't stolen my whiskey." He pulled in his line. "Damn, that's the sixth hook I lost today. Seems hooks are the one kind of food the fish around here will eat."

"That's because you keep giving them the best copper ones," the boy said. "You know they like those kind most and can live on them, in fact. Give them your bent-up rusty safety pins like I do and they'll taste one, spit it out, and leave your hooks alone from then on."

"What do you know about fishing anyway, son?" the man said. "Go back in the house and see if your ma needs any help with the ironing."

"I don't have a ma and I'm not your son. I first saw you when I came downriver on a canoe the pixies loaned me and you were fishing on this dock and called me over to stop."

"There are no pixies," I said.

"Who said there were?" the boy said. "All I'm saying is that before I came downriver, I also spoke to that inside man who said he was out, and before that fatted myself silly in a mountain I might have only dreamt I was in. And before that, I was on a three-legged horse who also couldn't have been the one either of you two rode, as this was a brown and black stallion named Just Plain Mo who'd only go east. And before that I was just too young to remember anything, something you two are too old to remember having been. But as far back as I can remember, I know the one thing I never was or wanted to be in my life was this man's son. And the one thing I never wanted to do for even a single hour in my life was fish off a dock with or without a mailbox on it and with any number of fish ready to be caught. And the one thing I was always trying to get to but never succeeded was California."

"That's where I'm heading for now," I said.

"California?" the boy said. "Where all those tall buildings are and the Catskill Mountains and Statue of Liberty and downtown New York?"

"That's New York State you want to go to and where I recently came from."

"That's not what my geography book says."

"He's right," the man said. "I seen him reading that book. It has all the facts you'd ever want in your life. And it says California is just what my boy here says."

"Believe me," I said. "If you look at that book again and see a map of a long American state with the Sierra Nevada on most of one side of it and the Pacific Ocean on all of the other side and that state isn't California, I'll buy you another geography book."

"Pacific Ocean?" the boy said, even more excited. "You mean the one with Coney Island and Cuba in it and those Cape Cod beaches and which is also called the Gateway to Europe?"

"That's the Atlantic Ocean. The Pacific is the one on just the other side of this country."

"Look at him," the boy said. "Doesn't even know that the state he's traveling to is California. But what do you say you take me along, mister? As my dream has always been to meet up with my sister under the Brooklyn Bridge."

"I'd love to. But the California I want to get to must be a different one than yours."

I was beginning to feel concerned for the boy with his pained expression and the harsh way his father treated him, so I said "If it's okay with your dad, why don't you come with me anyway? Because even if we reach my California on the Pacific, all we have to do is work for a while when we get there and then send you to your sister in your California in New York."

"Nah," the boy said. "I'm getting the feeling you don't know where either of our Californias is. Then you'll get us both lost and wind us up in some California in the middle of the country, so the best thing for me now is to stick right here," and he reeled in an empty line. "Think I better run back and ask Ma if dinner's ready?" he asked the man.

"What ma?" the man said.

"Then I'll run back to the house and get dinner myself."

"What house?"

"The one I caught for us last year that was coming downriver."

"You mean the one you tried to catch but couldn't keep. I told you your line wasn't long and strong enough and that you should let me help you bring it in with my tackle and rod. But no, you wouldn't listen to me. Thought you had become smarter than the old man. Said to me 'This baby's mine and mine alone, Pa, and nobody's getting credit for bringing it in but me,' and you let get by us the biggest darn house we ever seen floating down this river. From now on I don't want you calling me Pa or Pop or any of those words, you hear? Because just thinking of that house fished out farther downriver by a lesser fisherman who probably won't even know what to do with his catch, makes me ashamed you're my son."

"I'm not your son and you're not my father."

"That's right. You aren't and I'm not. But next don't go forgetting what you just said to me here either, as this man's my witness."

"Beg your pardon, sir," I said. "I don't want to be causing any bad blood between you two. And I don't see how I can be your witness for very long, as I've got to get a move on soon."

"Don't worry your head none, as bad blood between this boy and me started long before you arrived. And if I suddenly need you as a witness, then just like I done with this boy here, I can find you and bring you back anytime I please."

"Then you'll have to stick pretty close and move right along with me," I said. "Though I don't mind company when I travel, I've still a long ways to go and am going to get there fast as I can."

The man and boy resumed their fishing. I began this letter, will stick it in the dock mailbox when I'm through writing it, and leave.

Always your friend,
Rudy

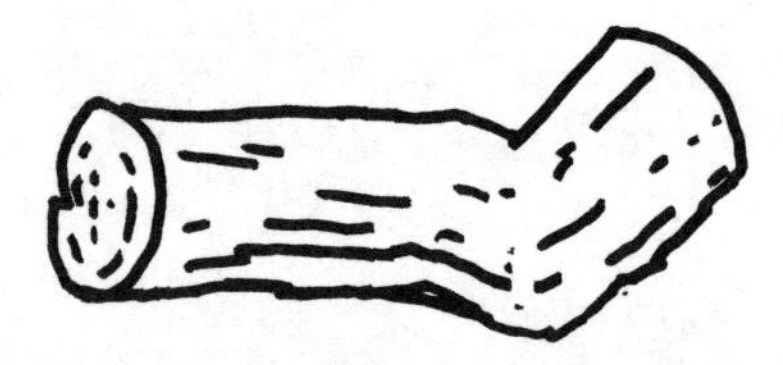

Dear Kevin:

I said goodbye to the man and boy, went down a path, came to a country road and walked along it, hoping to meet someone who could direct me to a highway. After a few miles without seeing anyone, I sat on a log. The log rolled forward soon as I sat on it, and I fell on my back with my head bouncing off a rock.

Loose log, I thought. I sat more carefully on the log next to it. This one rolled backward so fast that I fell on my face.

"Couple of logs that don't want to be sat on," I said, laughing at such a ridiculous thought. I tore my handkerchief in half to dab the cuts on my head and lip, and started off again searching for a highway. A few minutes later I heard bumping sounds behind me. When I looked back I didn't see anything but a couple of logs and lots of loose twigs and stones off the road, but nothing moving.

I continued walking and heard these same bumping sounds behind me. This time I turned around quickly and saw two logs bouncing along. They dropped to the ground the moment I saw them, and rolled off the road and made a dead stop at the side, as if they were just two ordinary logs that had been there since they were cut up from a fallen tree a while ago.

"You two following me?" I said.

The logs, each about two feet long and round and wide as a dinner plate, said nothing.

"Sure," I said, standing over them. "You're only waiting to be hollowed out by termites for a chipmunk's home. Because logs can't talk just as they can't walk, am I right?"

Of course logs can't talk, I thought. They can't walk either.

I must have been seeing things. Maybe losing my marbles altogether from being without sleep so long. What I need is a long snooze, and I lay on the side of the road and rested my head on one of the logs.

The log rolled away from me as I was dozing off, and my head hit the ground again. I got up and kicked the log, as my head really hurt from the banging. The log jumped up on one of its ends and hobbled around as if I had hurt it badly. Then it bumped into the woods.

The other log stood on its end and jumped higher and higher till it got up to about half my size, when it swung at me with its top end but missed. It fell on its side, as if it had lost its footing from jumping so high and swinging at me so clumsily. Then it bumped into the woods after the first log.

"Least I got rid of them." I walked on. After a minute or so I heard bumping sounds from inside the woods next to the road. This time it was like two heavy objects bumping on broken branches and dried leaves instead of the bumping thumping sounds of logs on a packed-down road.

"You logs in there still trailing me?" I said, feeling that since I couldn't lose them, I better face them.

Two plops, one after the other, were the next sounds I heard. These were probably the logs diving to the ground and pretending to be ordinary abandoned logs in the woods, though I couldn't see them.

"Well, come on out and say or do what you've in mind to. As I swear not to be rough again, if you won't with me."

They bumped out of the woods onto the road.

"Now why you following me?" I said, and they bounced up and down a few times, which made no sense to me.

"Because you think I'm lost and want to lead me out?"

They bounced up and down faster.

"I'm sorry, I no understand log language too good. So if your next answer is 'yes,' try bouncing only once for it. And if it's 'no,' bounce twice, okay?" They bounced once.

"Fine. Now you are following me?" and they bounced once.

"Why?" and they bounced three times. This was way beyond me, as the only words in log language I knew were the ones I either made up or they had before I met them—one bounce for "yes" and two for "no."

"Look. Why don't we make three bounces mean 'I don't know'?" and they bounced twice.

"Three bounces already means something else in your language?" and they bounced once.

"If we're going to understand one another, we have to get the right number of bounces for 'I don't know.' Let's make it four."

They bounced twice.

"Five, then?" and they bounced once.

"Good, Then one bounce means 'yes.' Two 'no.' Three doesn't mean 'I don't know.' I've no idea what four bounces means. But five means 'I don't know.' Now. You two know your way pretty good around these woods, right?" and they bounced once.

"Great. Do you know a shortcut to a highway where I could get a bus or hitch to California?"

They bounced six times together, paused briefly, bounced three times and stopped.

"Too complicated. I don't even know what three bounces means yet. Do those six bounces plus the three mean that highways or buses don't run through here?"

They bounced eight times and stopped. Then one bounced twice. Then the other bounced ten times. Then both bounced nineteen times together, moving toward each other as they bounced till they nearly touched, then farther away from one another and stopped.

"I don't understand. Did all that bouncing and moving around mean a single sentence or statement in your language?"

They bounced once and tapped both ends.

"Both?" and they bounced once.

"I'm at least beginning to grasp some of your language," and they bounced once, paused, bounced twice.

"But not a whole lot, that what you're saying?"

They bounced once, fell to the ground and rolled over and got up and bunked their top ends once on the ground.

"What? I just said something insulting and you're mad? Or funny and you laughed?"

They bounced twice, stopped, bounced once.

"Tell me, though. Since one log uses the other to speak with, do you always stick together?" and they bounced once.

"What happens if one gets carted off or even rots away, heaven forbid?"

One log fell to the ground and stayed still. The standing log bumped and swayed till it fell on top of the log. Then it got up, scooped up earth with its bottom end till it covered the log on the ground with leaves and dirt. It then bumped in a circle around the log, repeatedly falling across the mound and getting up wobbling and bouncing twice. Then it circled the mound, but farther and farther away from it, falling here and swaying and staggering there, but always much less so, till I said "After everything's over including the mourning period, it looks for another log to be with?"

The log under the leaves jumped up beside the standing log, and the two tapped top ends together three times and bounced once.

"What are you? Male or female or mixed together something like that?" and they bounced once, stopped, twice, stopped, then once.

"Married?" and they bounced five times.

"How can I begin to explain it?" and they bounced three times.

"Three bounces means I should try explaining it?"

They bounced once. Then they knocked their top ends together, rolled completely over a few times and jumped up bouncing and tapped their top ends together.

"What? 'Hurray' because I finally found out what three bounces means?" and they bounced once.

"Okay. Now that we can speak together a little, I'll ask again if you know a shortcut to the highway, and if you do, where?"

They bounced twelve times together, weaving around one another as they bounced. Then one bounced six times, then the other. Then they bounced twenty-four times together, fell down, rolled back and forth a lot though not completely over, bunking each other at either end every other time. Then they got up, bounced fifty or so times, stopped, a hundred or so times and stopped, this time with their top ends leaning on one another.

"What did all that mean except for your being tired at the end?"

They went through the same long routine, though instead of ending up leaning on one another, they rolled off each other's top ends to the ground.

"You saying it's something I can't understand yet?"

They forced themselves up by leaning against one another as they rose, bounced once and fell down.

"Too bad," and from their flat positions they bounced one of their ends.

"Later, why not accompany me if you're heading my way?"

They got up, bounced five times and collapsed.

"'Accompany.' You know. To go with someone," and I bounced a few steps up the road, my feet coming down together each time.

They got up and bounced four times.

"I'm sorry, but those four bounces of yours I never figured out."

They bounced four times and stopped, repeated this four-bounces-and-stop number over and over till I said "I'm saying I still don't know. Does it mean 'to watch' or 'Listen!' or something?" and they bounced once, stopped, bounced about ten feet up the road together and turned around and bounced back.

"Then 'walking alone' is probably just one of you bouncing about ten feet and back?" and they bounced once.

"Well, this might be a more difficult verb to explain. But how do you say 'to sleep,' as I can see you're both as tired as I am," and they fell down and didn't move.

We slept the night by the road. In the morning we set off together, the logs chattering constantly to one another as we walked. Finally I said "Nice day, hey?" as I was getting dizzy with all their bouncing and falling and rolling around me which I couldn't understand. And also because I felt left out and wanted to learn more of their language for the time I was still with them.

They bounced twice, tapped their top ends against my knees once, and took a left at the crossroad we'd come to.

"Where you going?"

They bounced four times and went farther along the road.

"Well, it's sure been nice knowing you," and they fell down, rolled a little ways to me, rolled the same distance back, got up and bounced a bunch of bumps up the road without turning around again, and rolled into the woods.

"Wait. Which of these roads do I take?" and I ran after them.

In the woods were two other logs of the same kind of white birch tree as my couple, bouncing on the same spot faster and faster and then bouncing out to meet the logs whom I knew. When they met, they all bunked their top ends together once, so that they all touched at the same time. Then one of the logs whom I knew fell to the ground and the other log bunked its mate's middle very hard. When the log managed to stand again, the three other logs leaned on its top end for a while. Then the two couples bounced farther into the woods.

I followed them. Not only to later learn which might be the better road to avoid. But also because I've never been an expert on anything before. And here, out of the blue, I was becoming an expert on what was probably the one subject left that nobody was an expert on yet: the language, customs and behavior of logs.

They stopped bumping along after a mile, lay down like a plus sign with all four bottom ends meeting in the middle and stayed there for about an hour. Maybe that was how they rested up after what to them might have been a long journey. Or that could be the custom or even the latest fad among logs, to sleep that way after two couples of the same tree type had either met by accident or plan. But they eventually got up and began talking.

There must be sentences or topics in log language that can only be spoken through the combined movements and rest breaks of two couples instead of one. Or else some rule that forbids logs from speaking any other way but together once they meet. Because these two couples were always speaking in relation to one another and never gabbed on by themselves.

For instance, after one long stop, all four logs bounced up and down ten times. Then one log bounced six times while another log swung at it and the other two logs fell down and bunked their top ends. Then these two logs rolled around at the same time but in different directions, while the other two were bouncing to and away from one another but around the rolling logs. Then three logs all at once butted the fourth log to the ground and covered part of it with leaves. The buried log dug itself out, got up on the top end of another log and bounced up and down on it, while the other two logs rolled underneath them every time this double log bounced into the air.

Later, they walked a ways into the woods till they came to a lake. There, twenty-eight white birch logs of about the same length and thickness were bouncing in place faster and faster and then bumped and rolled out to meet them.

When the two groups met, they went through the same greeting as the two couples before. They got in a circle and bunked top ends together, getting as close as possible to having all their top ends touching or nearly touching at the same time. Then a log from the couple my couple had met before, rammed its top end into the middle of its mate. When the struck log managed to stand again, the other thirty-one logs fell on top of it. Then without getting up, all thirty-two logs rolled into the lake. They floated to the other side and back without splashing, so I couldn't tell whether logs speak in the water.

They all started talking at once when they returned to the

side I was on. Nine logs bounced together while six logs rolled around them and three logs tapped their tops on the ground and twelve of the remaining fourteen logs buried parts of the other two, and things like that.

I realized that log language gets more and more complicated with the number of logs added to the conversation. It could be the most complex language there is. Maybe impossible for anyone to learn completely unless he brought all the white birch logs of the world together and for a long time watched them speak.

It's also possible that only logs of the same tree that had been cut up into logs become couples. And that if one log loses its mate for some reason, it has to find a log from that same tree who has also lost its mate. Or one from the same tree who has always been alone and speechless before because it was cut last and became the odd log.

What I never learned for sure was how these couples arranged to meet here. It seemed that this information was carried from grove to grove in this forest by a couple of messenger logs. The log couple I first met, for example, as they were the only logs I saw on the road.

I didn't exactly know. These thoughts were mostly guesswork on my part, formed from the bits and pieces of conversation I was able to pick up from these thirty-two logs. The only thing I came closest to being a hundred percent sure about, was that all thirty-two logs were cut from the same tree. Not only from their conversations but because of their similar length, size around, condition of their bark and the way it peeled.

I followed the sixteen couples to a forest clearing where there were hundreds of white birch logs of various lengths, girths and bark conditions. The greeting ceremony between the two groups lasted an hour because of the difficulty of getting all their top ends as close to bunking one another as they could at the same time.

But the next greeting ceremony lasted half a day when five more groups of a few hundred logs each, came bouncing and rolling through the woods from different directions to join the meeting.

Their language became so complicated that I knew I'd never learn it in even a lifetime of watching them. All two thousand or so logs spoke at the same time. But to complete even the simplest sentence, about a hundred different movements were going on by separate groups and single couples and individual logs. Though whenever a stop came, it was made by all the logs together.

I now felt that this gathering was a convention of the elected representatives of all the white birch groves in this forest and the surrounding ones. When they weren't just chattering away, all the logs stood in neat long rows before four other logs. Every so often these rows bounced once or twice or five times together to some other kind of movement the four logs were making at the same time.

I thought that maybe these logs reset like this from time to time to work out problems that only white birch logs in this area have, such as a special insect blight or animal or human pests. Or perhaps this was one of many similar conventions being held by logs of all the white birch trees in this country or continent on whether to band together to declare war on the logs of another type birch tree. Maybe logs are the ones who start most forest fires—as an act of strategy against nature or war to wipe out every kind of log type but their own.

I also felt that as much as I wanted these questions answered and my guesswork checked out, I'd never let on I'd been following them. They might surround and stomp me if they learned I'd been watching them, afraid that any information leak about them could lead to mobs of people raiding the forests to use or sell them as pets. Or to put them in botanical garden cages so that the rest of us, who might not be so fortunate as I was to see them in their natural state, could go gaga and be educated and frightened and amused.

These logs might also fear that if their meeting grounds and possible war plans became known, another type of more numerous though less clever log might unite and attack them first, to destroy them as a potential danger to all the world's logs.

That evening every log fell to the ground at the same time and just stayed there, which I remember meant the words "to sleep." All the logs but three slept in many circles, one within another. In the center of all these circles, like a bull's eye in a target, two logs slept side by side with a third log lying on top between them.

I was tired also from no sleep for two days. I thought I'd doze off and wake up when they did and follow them till I had enough information and understanding about white birch logs to fill a book.

The logs were gone when I woke up. Not a trace of them, except for a trail of bouncing and rolling marks leading to me, around me and then to a river, where they must have floated away as a single group.

I tried retracing my steps back to the road where I first met the two logs, but was lost. I looked around for a couple of white birch logs to help me find my way out, since they were the only type log I could speak with. But none was around. I did trip over a three-foot-long oak log who was alone.

Maybe oak logs speak also, I thought. No oak log ever spoke to me before, though maybe because I never tried speaking with them first. So I looked for another oak log of about the same length and size around, and dragged it over to the first log.

"Excuse me," I said, "but you know how I can get out of this forest?"

They stayed there like the kind of logs I had always been used to till a few days ago: not moving, as if they didn't understand a word I said.

I sat on one. It didn't move. I rested my head on it and kicked it. Nothing. The other log didn't even jump up to protect the log I kicked.

Maybe oak logs don't need a second log to speak with. So I carried one away and said when I got it alone: "Listen, I'm sorry for kicking you before. But could you please tell me how to get out of here?" but it didn't move.

Maybe oak logs only speak in threes or fives or nines, instead of twos or ones. And whatever length, girth and bark conditions they are don't matter.

So I rolled over eight more oak logs of various sizes and tried speaking with them in every possible combination and number. I even stood two logs up while seven were resting. And then put one log on top of three logs while four others were standing and one was resting. Then I gathered all the oak logs in the area and piled them on top of one another in layers and threatened to set fire to the forty of them if they didn't speak. That still didn't work.

One thing I learned in my study of logs is a piece of information most everyone already knows: oak logs don't speak. Though I can say I'm probably the one person who's done thorough research on the subject. I even said in front of them "Well, I guess oak logs don't speak," and hid behind a bush and watched them for the rest of the day. I thought maybe they had had a big party or war of their own and were exhausted and sleeping it off and for that reason couldn't speak. But none of them bounced or rolled even once.

Maybe all logs but white birch speak without the logs actually moving. Silently and invisibly, like electric waves from each of them meeting and forming into couples or just bouncing, bunking, falling and rolling around together in the air. But rather than try and tune into this silent way of speaking, and maybe starving by then, or gathering even more logs of every size and type in this forest and arranging them in thousands of different combinations till the right one worked for them to speak, I started following the river the white birch logs had gone in.

I did stop to write this letter. I wanted to get down on paper my discoveries about white birch logs and the results of my experiments with other logs, before I forgot it all.

Yours sincerely,
Rudy

Dear Kevin:

I followed the river for three days and nights. Then I saw a plane overhead, heard a steam whistle from a ship, tripped over a railroad track and walked along the rails till I reached a city in Utah.

I was now only a few hundred miles from the California border and didn't see why I should have any trouble getting to you soon. I mailed my last letter and got on a train for San Francisco. The conductor came over and said "Ticket, please."

"I'm sorry," I said. "I didn't have time to buy one at the ticket window."

"You can buy one from me," and he punched out a ticket.

"I also didn't have time to withdraw money from the bank to buy a ticket."

"What did you have time for except to try and sneak a free train ride?"

"Do you mean in former times, in between times or for the time being?" I said.

"This won't be the first time in a long time that I haven't time to spend listening to your timeworn time-killing excuses about time till this train leaves on time. So can you spare ten seconds of your time to march double time out of this car?"

"Can you give me time to think about that?"

"Your time's up for all time here, chum. So off you go or in no time I'll have the time of my life seeing that you're doing time," and he edged me up the aisle and out of the train after it had begun moving.

"My typewriter," I yelled, running alongside the train.

He tossed it out the window. I luckily caught the typewriter by its case handle before it smashed on the ground.

"Bad timing on my part," the conductor yelled back.

In the city's business district I went to one of those U-Drive-It places where you can drive someone's car while the car owner takes the more relaxed trip out by train, ship or plane.

The U-Drive-It manager said "Sure, we got a car that needs driving to Palo Alto. But you got to give us a fifty-dollar deposit, which you get back from the car owner when you deliver the car to her safe and sound.

"I haven't fifty dollars."

"Borrow it from a loan company."

The loan company manager said "You got something to give us to hold that's worth fifty dollars till you pay back the loan?"

"Nothing but this typewriter which I wouldn't part with and isn't worth five bucks."

"Then borrow the fifty from a bank. Buy a car with that money, give us the car as security, and we'll give you a fifty-dollar loan."

I went to the bank. The bank manager said "We'll be happy to loan you fifty dollars. But you'll have to give us two credit references from either a bank or loan company that you've paid back two loans of at least fifty dollars each in the past three years."

"First loan me fifty dollars. With that money I can buy a car to give to the loan company as security for its fifty-dollar loan. I'll use that loan as the fifty-dollar deposit for the U-Drive-It office, which I'll get back from the car's owner in Palo Alto when I deliver the car to her. Then I'll buy a car with the fifty-dollar deposit she returns to me, drive back to this city, sell the car for fifty dollars, pay back the loan company its fifty-dollar loan and get back the car I gave them as security, and sell that car for fifty dollars and pay this bank back its fifty-dollar loan. Then I'll have the two credit references I need to show you I've paid back two fifty-dollar loans: the loan from the loan company and the one from this bank."

"When you have those two credit references," she said, "come see us anytime and we'll give you a fifty-dollar loan."

"I may have to. Because after I drive back here and sell those two cars and pay back both loans, I'll probably still want to return to Palo Alto in another U-Drive-It car. And for security to take out a loan from the loan company to get the fifty-dollar deposit for the U-Drive-It car, I'll have to borrow fifty dollars from this bank to buy a car."

I left the bank, still looking for a way to get to Palo Alto.

"Vote for Senator Bray," a lady on the street was shouting into a microphone. "A vote for Bray will give the people a say."

And there rumbling down Main Street was a truck with a long wagon attached to it, filled with waving and cheering people and posters, streamers and flags. Some of the people screamed "Climb on the bandwagon" and "Bray's the man, so get on while you can."

I asked the lady what this all meant. She said "Senator Bray is running to be his party's candidate for president. Though no one thought he had a chance to win, he now seems the man all the other candidates must beat."

"Is the bandwagon going to California?"

"Right to it, straight through it, smack down the middle of it, then all around it a few times before it starts back across the country to the East Coast."

"Then he's the candidate for me."

I climbed on the bandwagon, was given a mimeograph machine to run, a cold fried chicken wing to eat, a pennant to wave and a leaflet which said for everyone to chant in unison "A vote for Bray is a voice for a new day." And I began to copy, chew, wave and chant at the same time.

The bandwagon went from city to city and always more and more people climbed on. Like everyone else aboard, I didn't see how the wagon could stop moving till Bray had become his party's candidate for president.

After four days of traveling through Utah and Nevada and almost reaching the California border, a newspaper was passed around whose headlines read "Bray Loses Two State Primaries. No Longer Considered Serious Candidate," and right then and there the bandwagon got a flat.

Everyone jumped off. A few walked away, but most sat on the other side of the road eating the last box lunches the wagon had. I was the only one who figured that if the flat was fixed, the bandwagon could start moving again. So I asked Senator Bray for a jack and lifted the back of the wagon to put on a spare tire.

"At least there's still two of us who believe I can be the winning candidate," he said.

"I don't know much about politics, sir. But if your wagon's going to California, I want to be on it."

"Makes no difference how strong or what your political beliefs are, just so long as you're for me. Now let's get this buggy rolling again."

He sat in the driver's seat. I got on the wagon part and he yelled for me to turn the tape recorder on. It blasted out the message "To end all wars and double your pay, you gotta climb back on and this time stick with Bray." But we were out of gas.

"Loan me a dollar for gas, son," he said. "My campaign fund's done run dry."

I turned out my empty pockets and pointed to the rope and pins I now used to hold up my pants.

"Hock your typewriter," he said. "We can get twenty gallons for it, which will take us right to that town you want to reach."

I wrestled my typewriter away from him and crossed the road.

"Maybe one of these cars whipping by me can spare some gas," he said. "I'm sure I can make it to California and back East again if all the drivers who are for me pitch in with a single gallon apiece."

Just then we heard loud honking and band music and garbled pep talk from what seemed like a huge circus van tearing down the hill toward us from California.

"It's Governor Flay's bandwagon," someone said. "The candidate who beat Bray in those two state primaries and whom everyone now thinks is the man of the day who's going all the way."

Flay's wagon was much bigger and newer than Bray's and had hundreds of applauding people on board and many more banners, microphones and a live band. It stopped in front of us. All the people around me who had been on Bray's wagon climbed on Flay's.

Governor Flay reached over the wagon to Senator Bray and me and said "Give me your hands while you can, boys. We're going clear through to New York and then to the White House in D.C."

"Wrong direction for me," I said, "but thanks."

Senator Bray climbed on, raised Flay's hand above their heads and said "Bray's choice for today is the great Governor Flay."

And with the band blaring and people hurraying, the wagon roared off for New York.

I was too near Palo Alto to turn around now. I stuck a few discarded chicken necks in my pockets and put my thumb out for a ride.

The first thing on wheels to come along was a state trooper on a motorcycle. He said "Hitchhiking' s illegal in this state," and wrote out a ticket.

I said "I wasn't hitchhiking. Just walking along the road to California and sticking my thumb out to see if the wind was blowing hard enough to carry me part of the way."

"Now walking and feeling which way the wind's blowing is legal in this state. But any questionable-looking person passing through has got to prove he's not a vagrant. And in this state, a vagrant's a vagabond with no money in his pockets."

"I don't carry my money in my pockets. I keep it in my shoes, as I've fewer holes there than in my pockets."

I took off my shoes to show him the change I'd picked up from the campaign contributions that had fallen under the floorboards in Bray's wagon and which I found when Bray left and the wagon collapsed and the floorboards fell off. But he was already writing out a second ticket for my not having any money in my pockets.

"Get three tickets in any one day in this state and we bring you up before the judge."

"Don't worry, officer. Getting as close to my destination as I am, I'm not about to do anything unlawful from now on and get thrown in jail."

"Then you can pay for these tickets?"

I gave him all the money that was in my shoes.

"Seems enough. But I'll have to write out another ticket for your now not having any money on you, which makes you a vagrant."

He wrote it out, counted the tickets, said "Why it seems to add up to exactly enough to take you to the judge," and put me on the back of his motorcycle and rode to the trooper station.

All the cells there were full. The trooper captain said "Let's just throw the bum out of the state and be done with him." Three troopers picked me up, shoved me into a car and drove to the state line and threw me into Arizona.

Right over the state line was an Arizona trooper who said "Jumping the border's illegal in this state. I'll have to bring you in."

"I didn't jump. I was thrown."

"That's okay then. But anyone entering Arizona has to have some visible means of support."

"I have it," as I spotted a quarter on the ground. I grabbed it and put it in my pocket, in case Arizona also had a law which said that vagabonds must have money in their pockets. But the quarter dropped through the hole in my pocket and rolled away, just as I was about to ask the trooper for a needle and thread to sew up that hole.

"There it is," I said, pointing to where I heard the quarter rolling.

"I can hear it but I can't see it," the trooper said. "So I'll have to arrest you for having no visible means of support."

"How can I be arrested for having something I don't have?" but he drove me to the courthouse.

The judge I was brought before said "Let's save the taxpayers the cost of a jail term for this tramp and throw him out of the state.

Four troopers picked me up, carried me to the state line and threw me back into Nevada.

Some Nevada troopers were waiting for me there and threw me back into Arizona.

"If Nevada won't have him," the Arizona troopers said, "we'll throw the stiff into the next state from ours on the other side.

PLAY

They drove me in a paddy wagon to the state line touching New Mexico and threw me over the border.

"You're much better off here," a New Mexico trooper said, helping me up. "Drifters are allowed to roam throughout the state free and clear. But I'll have to book you for entering New Mexico without first registering as a convicted criminal with a record in two states, Arizona and Nevada."

The local magistrate in town said "I've conned enough shifty deals for one day. I mean, I've dealt with enough shiftless cons for today. Throw the hobo out of the state on his ear."

The troopers were much rougher with me this time because of my growing criminal record, and tossed me over the state line into Texas on my ear.

A Texas state trooper was about to arrest me for having no visible means of support, no money in my pockets or shoes, and for trying to enter Texas without first registering as an ex-convict with convictions in three states, when I heard Governor Flay's bandwagon rumbling through the desert.

This time when the governor reached over the side and said "Climb aboard, neighbor, there's room for one more," I got on. Because what was the sense in being tossed from state to state on my ears? Till I was tossed all the way across America this way and ended up with two frazzled ears, no earlobes, a mangled typewriter, several filthy chicken necks in my pockets and a criminal record so long that I might not be thrown over the New York State border when I got there, but into a prison cell for thirty years.

So I stayed with Flay. Worked his mimeograph machines. Handed out his leaflets and shopping bags. Chanted his slogans and listened to his paid political advertisements and waved his flags.

By the time the bandwagon reached New York City, Flay had collected enough delegate votes to be chosen his party's candidate for president, and most polls were calling him a shoo-in for the job. He asked me to run his mimeograph machines all the way to the White House. But I got off in Brooklyn, walked across the bridge to Manhattan, and found a clean quiet doorway in my old neighborhood to sleep the night.

Before I fell asleep I began writing this letter. I'll drop it in a mailbox when I'm done. If you do get the letter, you'll know how close I got to Palo Alto this time. And that I now have enough mimeograph-machine experience to join up with another candidate's bandwagon going to California in four years, if I can't get out there before then on my own.

Best,
Rudy

Dear Kevin:

I had the most unbelievable dream last night as I slept in that doorway.

In the dream I woke up in my old apartment, washed and dressed, had breakfast and packed a small suitcase and locked the front door. I took a subway to Times Square and the subway shuttle to 42nd Street and the East Side. I walked the few blocks to the airline bus terminal, took the bus to Kennedy Airport and bought a ticket on the next plane flying to San Francisco. I had lunch on the plane, napped, and woke as we were landing. I took the airport limousine to Palo Alto. In Palo Alto I cabbed to your house.

I rang your bell. You opened the door. "Surprise," I said. "Rudy," you said. We kissed and hugged. I gave you a present. You took me to the kitchen where your mother was having tea.

"Who was at the door?" she said.

"Surprise," both you and I said.

We all kissed and hugged, I gave her a present. "You shouldn't have," she said.

"But you're glad he did," you said.

Your mother and you led me to the backyard where your dog Saybean was. Saybean put out his paw. "Shake," you said to Saybean and me. I shook his paw. We all laughed, grabbed hands and danced in a circle around Saybean, who barked happily and danced inside our circle by holding his tail between his teeth. The dream ended. A really unbelievable dream, I thought. Maybe sleeping in doorways is good for that.

In real life I woke up when someone poked my cheek with a wine bottle. It was an old man. Clothes as ragged as mine, face as much in need of a shave. He offered me a drink.

"No thanks," I said, brushing off my clothes. "Got to keep a clear head and steady pace if I'm to get to California in the next four years."

"California? Why I got just what you want."

"Sure you do. Everybody does," and I walked away.

He clutched my elbow and wrote the address of a man in New York who he said has a trapdoor in his basement. "Now this door doesn't just go down to his workshop. But to a hand-built two-man submarine that travels under the Atlantic Ocean and St. Lawrence Seaway and Great Lakes to Chicago, where it then goes by uncharted underwater waterway to the San Francisco Bay."

“No more schemes,” I said. “Because none of them work. Only way to get to Palo Alto is to go like I did in last night’s dream. I buy a ticket, fly to San Francisco, take the airport limousine to Palo Alto and cab to this boy’s home.”

“If you got all the money for that, do it.”

“I haven’t. But starting right now I’m going to find me some better rags, get a crummy job, rent a cheap flat, buy better second-hand clothes, get a better-paying job and save up enough money in a few years to buy a plane ticket to San Francisco and pay for the limousine and cab to Kevin’s house.”

“And where will you sleep nights till you get the security deposit and first month’s rent for your cheap flat?”

“On that subway grating. In this doorway. But some place equally warm and clean.”

“And your shaves and baths?” he said. “Your wrinkled clothes? You’ll wake up looking and smelling like a grizzly bear. And maybe get arrested for impersonating a derelict. You think then you could find a job? No chance. Take the submarine.”

“I’ll get a hotel room and keep my clothes and me clean that way.”

“Get a hotel room and your whole salary will be spent for food and rent. Come on. What’s to lose? And I know a way to get you the ride free.”

“Sure.” I said. “A free submarine ride straight under the states to San Francisco.”

“Not so straight. A little curve here. A big dip there. More like a winding hilly road in the water, as it follows Interstate 80 once it leaves from Chicago. But always under the earth, when there are no rivers and lakes to go in, and it never comes up till the end. It’ll get you there in ten to fifteen days maximum, depending on the currents and weather conditions below. Now what do you say?”

"Pardon me," I said, trying to step around him. "As I really got to start checking the trash cans for clothes."

"Took the same ride myself several times," he said. "And always free because I always answered the same three questions this kind of eccentric submarine captain makes you answer to get his rides for nothing. So there's a hundred percent chance you'll get the ride free, if I tell you the answers and some other passenger doesn't get to him first."

I walked away. He caught up with me and put his arm around my shoulder.

"First question the captain will ask you," he said, "is 'How many fingers do we have altogether?' Now you look like a pretty clever guy. So naturally you'll give his hand the once over and see nine. And then count your own fingers and find ten. And nine and ten makes for nineteen. So you'll say to him: 'We got nineteen fingers altogether.'"

"Wow, that was a mind-grinding question."

"But you'd be wrong, smart guy. Because the answer to 'How many fingers do we got altogether?' is 'Ten.' Because Dewey is the name of his son. And Dewey's only got ten fingers, understand?"

"You bet," I said, digging out yesterday's newspaper from a trash can. I dumped the coffee grounds wrapped inside and opened the paper to the Help Wanted section. Unless, in the next few hours, I could gain five years' experience in inventory and production control or master the alphanumeric punch and verify system of a 360 DOS/OS computer, there were no jobs for me.

"Now the second question he'll ask for his free submarine ride," the man said, "is 'What's the color of green peas?'"

"Cooked, parboiled or raw?"

"Wrong. Though most people, you'd be surprised to know, would have said 'Green.' As green peas are green just as yellow canaries are yellow, right? But they'd also be wrong with their answer 'Green.' Because Green Peas is the name of Dewey's yellow canary. So you've got to give 'Yellow' as your answer to the second question, got it?"

"Exactly. When the captain asks 'How many fingers do we got altogether?' I say 'Yellow.' And when he says 'What's the color of green peas?' I say 'Nineteen fingers.'"

"Okay, big shot. But another joke like that and I don't tell you the third question and answer."

"Now there's a big loss." I turned to the newspaper's Rooms for Rent section to see if there might be a hotel that would give me a few months' credit for my room, meals, laundry and shoe repairs while I looked for a job.

"The third and final question the captain will ask is 'Who's considered the father of our country?' It would of course be too easy to say 'George Washington' to that one, right?"

"I suppose so," I said.

"You suppose so? After those last two questions, you'd have to assume that this one was tricky too. So I'd think you'd be smart enough to say to the captain 'Well. Since *do we* turned out to be your son Dewey. And *green peas* turned out to be Dewey's yellow canary. Then *our country* in that last question is probably the name of a pet monkey or dog or some animal like that.'"

"You might have a point."

"I might? How dumb can you be? I'm trying to tell you the answer can't be just 'George Washington.' The captain's not giving these free trips to the first person who asks for it, you know. Because his are the rarest of rides. A trip any traveler in the know would swindle a fortune to take. So thinking 'our country' is the name of a dog or something, you'd probably come up with a popular name for one, like Rover or Spot. And you might think long and hard on these two and settle on Spot. Because maybe Spot rhymes with rot, which boats are prone to.

So you'd say to the captain 'Spot's considered the father of Our Country,' right?"

"Right."

"Well, you'd be wrong again, because 'Our Country' is the name of Dewey's cat and Green Peas's worst enemy. And the father of Our Country just happens to be a scruffy tom named George Washington. So if you had been smart enough to say 'George Washington' to begin with, you would have had the right answer and your free ride sewed up."

"I got it now," I said. "'Ten', 'Yellow' and 'George Washington.' All I have to do is give them in that order and I win one free underwater ride to the part of Palo Alto that's on the San Francisco Bay."

"I said nothing about the extra miles to Palo Alto. That you'd have to work out with the captain. But very comfortable quarters he has also. Gourmet meals. Movie theater. Game and exercise room. Library. All sorts of incredible sea creatures to see from your bedroom's bubbletop observation glass and through your bathtub. Only chores are to wash your dishes and make your bed. But that's all. A very safe trip. He practically invented the term 'under-America American submarine ride.' Now what do you say? I'd take the trip myself, but I don't know a soul in California anymore. And I'll walk you to the captain's house."

"Truth is," I said, "your story about the captain is the biggest chunk of bunk and baloney I've run across in a dog's age. What do you take me for, a dumb ox?" I pushed him aside and headed for a hotel along the docks which a newspaper ad said would give me free bed and board if I cleaned all the rooms and halls.

The man hobbled after me, grabbed my newspaper and slapped me on the head with it.

"Dumb ox," he screamed. "Dunce. First-class junkhead and second-class jerk. You can tell me the captain and his sub aren't real when in the past month you've spoken to pixies and logs and ridden a three-legged horse named Mo?"

"Just Plain Mo. And it's a proven fact that there has never been documented proof that pixies existed in any civilization or historical age."

"I know. You saying I said they ever did? But I'm living proof, just as you're soon to be, that the captain and his sub are as real as you and me."

He took my hand, and old and weak as he looked, dragged me against my will to a house at the end of this street by the river's edge. The house, made of steel, was shaped and painted like the raised part of a submarine periscope.

"And how'd you know about me and the logs and stuff?" I said.

He lifted a porthole in the door and said into it "Yo ho, blow the tank." Then he saluted me, said "Have a spiffy crossing, matey, and give your best to the adorable Aunt Belle Mae de Momma Devine," and sprinted around the corner.

"I said how'd you know about the logs, you lying phony? You big fake. Because there isn't any captain. And the only subs you've ever seen were those replacement teachers you used to taunt to tears in grade school because you were too chicken to razz your regular ones."

The door he left me before opened.

"Aye?" a man said. He had on a navy captain's suit and cap and held a cage with a yellow canary inside, which was being pawed and hissed at by the cat perched on his shoulder. "Down, Our Country," he said.

"You a submarine captain?" I said.

"At your service, sir."

"And you give free rides to San Francisco under America if the correct answers to your questions are given by a person who only then might decide to become your passenger?"

"Come to the point."

"Fire away then, captain. I'm ready."

"First question," he said, "is what floor does my Aunt Belle Mae de Momma Devine live on in her high-rise tenement house in Tashkent, Uzbekistan?"

"I was wondering what that guy who brought me here said about giving my best to her."

"Correct. Second question is how many pages are there still left in the world of all the books ever printed before and after the Mazarin Bible of 1456, though not including the Mazarin Bible or any book printed anywhere today?"

"You joking?" I said. "Nobody could answer that."

"Right. Third question is what was the exact hour and date of the last time I had my galley painted, how many coats were put on, and what color did I originally choose?"

"Hold it a second. I was told you'd ask three different questions than these."

"You're right. Ready for the fourth question?"

"I thought there'd only be three."

"Right again. You're doing fine. What do you think the fifth question will be?"

"How the heck should I know?"

"Splendid. You answered my five questions precisely right. Now when do you want to leave?"

"Is that your sixth question?"

"That's right. Can't fool you. You answered it correctly too. Would you like to be underway tonight?"

"Is that your seventh question?"

"That your seventh answer?"

"And was that your eighth question?"

"That your eighth answer to it?"

"It was."

"And that was my ninth question. Shall we go?"

"Let me think a moment what my answer should be."

"Don't bother, you've just given it. Now are we off or not?"

"I'm stumped on that last one."

"No need to be, as I only give ten questions."

"Then let's get started right away," I said.

"Wonderful. Can you hold my cage?"

"I'm sorry, but I'm allergic to birds."

"Good thing also. As I actually do give eleven questions and you just answered the eleventh perfectly." He set the cage down on the doormat and went into the house.

"You leaving the canary outside?" I said.

"I can't take it with us. She has very bad sea legs and her ears don't pop when we submerge. But she'll be okay. My wife Wilma will be home shortly, and the bird's legally hers."

"I thought it was your son Dewey's."

"We don't have a son Dewey, do you?"

He led me to the basement, lifted a rug up and opened a trapdoor beneath. We climbed down a ladder and through the conning tower of his waiting submarine. He sealed the hatch and told me to sit tight and comfort Our Country till we were safely out to sea and could surface. Then he spun a number of hand wheels and worked several panelboards of switches, buttons and circuit breakers, while he shouted at Our Country and me "Rig for diving...

Ventilate inboard... Flood main ballast... Pound in after trim and secure the main induction," and we were underway.

There isn't much to say about the voyage. It took thirteen days. The food was always cooked in its can by the captain and served cold. Once we left the Atlantic for the St. Lawrence Seaway, we were underground or underwater all the time. There were no books. I slept a lot, looked after the cat, and watched videos of the same three war movies over and over again, on a tiny TV screen. I eventually knew the dialogue so well that for something else to do, I ran the films silent and spoke all the parts. And then only played the films' soundtracks and acted out all the roles, including the radiotelegraph sets. Throughout the trip there was nothing to see in the periscope but the same pink eye of a very large fish looking back. And nothing to see through the bubbletop glass from my bedroom and bathtub but the body of that one-eyed fish who was either swimming along with us or got caught on something the whole way.

Starting from Chicago, a New York newspaper was dropped down a snorkel every morning in time for our breakfast. It was my job to fetch the paper from the intake tube and cut out for the captain all the articles about shipping and the sea. I once asked who was delivering the newspaper. He said "Who do you think?

Newsboys who pitch it with perfect aim at our snorkel as they ride by above on their bikes."

I said "You're of course not saying it's newsboys who are delivering it, right?"

"No," he said. "Instead it's a porpoise with an octopus on her back, which she has dunking the newspaper down to us after they finish reading it, Ach, how little you landlubbers know about snorkeling and seamanship."

One day I asked him how he had come upon this extraordinary route to the Pacific.

He said "I was in Lake Michigan near Chicago one night and got lost underwater when I fell asleep at the controls. When I finally could surface again without smashing the conning tower on the land overhead, I found myself in the San Francisco Bay. 'So, Captain,' I told myself then. 'You've discovered a transcontinental route more important than anything Balboa or Lewis and Clark found, except you don't know how you got here.' To find that same route again I first had to go down the California coastline and through the Panama Canal and back up to the St. Lawrence Seaway and into Lake Michigan. There, at the same site where I fell asleep at the controls months before, I blindfolded myself and submerged. I hoped I would get lost underwater again and end up in the San Francisco Bay. But it wasn't that easy. Trial and error, that's what serious exploration is. Plenty of dead ends, broken conning towers and underground rivers that sometimes led me back to where I was weeks before. Till one day I was in the Bay and could actually chart how I got there and how I could return to Lake Michigan through the same route."

"Why haven't you told the Navy of this? I'm sure they'd love to know of a shorter submarine route to the Pacific and Atlantic than under the North Pole."

"If I told them, my route would be too crowded for me to go to

San Francisco whenever I liked. Because it's very narrow in places. Over some stretches, there's room for only one small sub at a time."

Anyway, we got to California without trouble. We surfaced in the inlet off the San Francisco Bay where the Palo Alto Yacht Club connects up with the Palo Alto dump. The captain opened the hatch, said "Permission to leave is granted, Mr. Foy," and asked if he should wait for me for the return trip home.

"I think I'll be staying a while, but many thanks."

"I hate going back alone. Maybe I'll place an ad in the newspaper here for a return passenger. Though I don't see how anyone will ever be as clever again to answer those impossibly tough questions I insist on asking for the ride."

"Get someone to give out the questions beforehand," I said. "Like that man tried to do with me."

"Why not the man himself?"

He took off the captain's cap and put it in his pocket, took out of his other jacket pocket a folded-up fedora and put it on his head. Then he turned his jacket inside out, where it became a shabby windbreaker with a wine bottle sticking out of a side pocket, put the windbreaker on and pulled off a thin rubber mask I didn't know he'd been wearing all this time, and threw the mask into the water.

And there, standing on the conning tower and waving at me, was the same man who gave me the three wrong answers to the captain's eleven questions thirty-one days ago.

"It's been you all along," I said. "Well, what I'd still like to know, sir, is how you knew about me and those pixies and logs and such?"

He put the fedora back in his pocket, reversed the jacket and put the captain's cap on his head, pulled off the man's full-faced mask and threw it in the water, and underneath was the captain's face again.

"Captain," I said. "First of all I want to thank you for a most enjoyable voyage. Secondly—"

The captain switched hats, reversed the jacket, pulled off the captain's mask and took a swig from the wine bottle and became the man again.

"Oh there you are," I said. "Well, I'd still like to know who tipped you off about those logs and pixies and me."

He switched hats and jackets and pulled off the mask of the man and threw it in the water and became the captain again.

"Secondly, Captain," I said, "is a complaint, though a minor one, about why you couldn't provide better grub for supper but carrots and canned buttered rolls. Now for the meals on your return trip, might I suggest—"

But he kept switching hats and jackets and pulling off the masks one after the other and throwing them in the water. Soon he was switching outfits so fast that at times he was the man wearing the captain's hat and trying to put his arm in both sleeves of his jacket and other times he was the captain, guzzling from the wine bottle, with the man's mask on his head and jacket and hats sticking out of his pants pockets.

He only had two hats, but the masks he pulled off seemed to be endless. Maybe he started out wearing more than a hundred masks. And under the last one, which could be of either the captain or man, was the real face of the captain or man or of someone else.

Or maybe there wasn't a face under the last mask, but just one of those two hats on top of the high turtleneck collar covering his neck. And the real face was where his neck seemed to be. And the real neck was where his chest seemed to be and his chest was where his stomach seemed to be, and so on. Till his thighs were where his shins seemed to be and his shins were in his shoes where his feet would normally be. But then where would his feet be if his shins were inside his shoes?

"Goodbye, Captain," I said, when he seemed to settle on the real face of the captain and the captain's clothes.

"Goodbye, my boy. And keep in touch."

He pulled the mask off, switched hats and reversed jackets, but seemed too exhausted to stick his arms in the sleeves or straighten the fedora from its sideways position on his head.

"Then goodbye, sir," I said. "It's been nice knowing you both."

"Same here," the man said, "And best of luck to you."

He reversed the jacket, but only held it on his arm. Leaned forward to let the fedora fall off his head, slowly peeled off the mask to become the captain again, and smashed the bottle against the side of the conning tower and climbed down the ladder. From inside the tower he yelled "Stations for diving... Flood main vents... Shift the control and steady so and land ho and ahead," and closed the hatch and the sub soon submerged.

I walked to your house a couple miles away. Nobody seemed to be around. I rang the bell, knocked on the door, called out your name and your mom's, but still no one answered. I at least thought your dog Saybean would bark or run up to me and knock me over, though maybe you'd taken him for a stroll.

WAFER

I looked through all the windows. The furniture was gone. Not even a curtain rod remained. I checked the mailbox to see if you might have left a note for me where you had gone. The box was stacked with mail. Included were all the letters I had written to you since I first tried to call and then got locked inside a telephone booth in New York a long time ago.

I went next door. Your neighbor there, Mrs. Spinks, said you and your mom moved two months ago and left no forwarding address.

"Surely someone's got to know where they went," I said. "I've come a long ways. Gone through a swarm of troubles to get here. It's just not like Kev to slip off for even a few weeks' vacation without first writing to let me in on his plans."

"Something very odd did happen," she said. "Mr. Spinks and I haven't told the story to anyone for a while now, as everyone we told it to thought we'd gone out of our minds. You see, Mr. Foy, Kevin and his mother didn't move out of their house as plain ordinary folks would. You know: renting or selling their house and then filling a moving van with their belongings and getting in their car the last day and waving goodbye to their neighbors as they drove away. Oh no. Nothing was ever done about selling or renting the house, and you can see how the weeds have taken over and given our street a bad name. And as for their leaving. Well, they had to send all their belongings off by spaceship a week before they and their dog Saybean took off for space themselves."

"That's ridiculous," I said.

"You see? Nobody believes us. But do you want to hear what happened to them or not?" and I told her I did.

"Kevin used to drop by here quite often. We loved seeing him, as he was always so cheerful and bright. But one day, when I'm making him an ice-cream cone out of the freezer, he says to me that his best friend at school is a glouter flace gerson. 'A what?' I said, and he says 'A glouter flace gerson. That's an outer space person in the Giffiggof language they speak in their country on the planet my friend comes from.'

"Then he says that his friend and his family have been living in California for five years. Working as industrial spies here for their country, which is why they look, speak and dress like us earth people when they're on the outside. But when they're inside their homes, they act and look much differently than us. And also speak this different language, where all the words start off with G's and F's. 'I know,' he said. 'I've been in their house and gotten so close to them that they now think of me as their brother and son.'

"I asked where he'd heard such a story. He said 'It isn't a story.' And that very evening he was going to introduce his glouter flace griend and his griend's farents to his fom.

"As you can imagine, I quickly forgot about it. To me, it was only another wild concoction that Kevin's been entertaining us with for years and which we loved him for. But the next week, when I'm making him an ice-cream float on our soda fountain downstairs, he says how his mother has fotten griendly with these flace geeple. How she's even glinking of their both glying off with these geeple in a flace glip to their country on that other flanet, when the flace gamily's spy tour of guty on gearth is gup.

"I said 'Kevin, you ought to be writing science fiction for children with your imagination. Or telling these tales to an older-person writer, so she can type them up and try and get them published for you. Not that I don't love listening to you, dear. It's only that you can't expect me to believe every single word.'

"He shrugged his shoulders and said 'If we do go, Mrs. Spinks, I'll be sure to drop over to say goodbye to you and Mr. Spinks, as you've both been real kind to me.' I told him what a mature thing that was for a young boy to be saying, and he just sucked up his soda and left with his dog.

"I still didn't think anything of his stories till a few nights later when I was awakened by a crackling and humming noise outside. I looked out our bedroom window and saw a contraption such as I've never seen before. It was as long and had the looks and lines of a new silver stretch limousine. Except it had glass tubes and exhaust pipes sticking out on both sides of its bottom, and rotary blades on top, and it was settling down in their backyard.

"Then these creatures about the size of Kevin came out of it. They were dressed in dark overcoats that dragged on the ground and were buttoned up to their necks, and on their heads were what looked like baseball caps on backwards. Four of them went into Kevin's house through the rear entrance and were soon carrying out boxes and lamps and dishes and things to their flying limousine. By the time I woke up Mr. Spinks and found his glasses so he could see straight, the spaceship had floated above our house without the blades spinning or making noise. Then it slipped off into the night, the blades now humming and tubes glittering and pipes flashing fire fast as can be.

"Mr. Spinks wouldn't believe what I told him I saw—the first time in our thirty-year marriage he's done that. He did suggest I not listen to Kevin's tall stories anymore, as they were taking over my dreams and causing me to wake him from a deep sleep.

"But the next night it was Mr. Spinks who was awakened by these crackling and humming sounds. We both hunted for his glasses and saw a much larger spaceship land. And there again were these tiny people, now carting the heavier furniture out of Kevin's house into the ship. This time Kevin and his mother came outside to wave goodbye to the creatures waving at them from the pilot seat. And then, quietly as before, the spaceship floated up and, like a light, flew off.

"The next day Mr. Spinks and I hinted to Mrs. Wafer what we'd seen the previous night. She laughed and said 'I can't understand how two supposedly sane adults can believe in flouter glace flips or flacer glout fligs or whatever you called them landing in my backyard.'

"'Glouter flace glips,' I told her. 'And what about your furniture, Theresa? From what I can make out through your window, all you have left is a table and two chairs and a double sleeping bag.'

"'I've joined a new back-to-earth movement,' she said, 'and can't stand my old stuff. From now on Kevin and I are going to rough it and eat out of coconut shells and live off the floor. As for the strange noises you heard last night, a friend drove by in a dilapidated truck to take away everything I own.' And then, already red in the face from embarrassment from lying, I'm sure, she excused herself to go in her house.

"Two nights later, the smaller flace glip landed and this time Mr. Spinks called the police. By the time they came, these creatures had taken the table and two chairs and the glip was gone. We told the police what we saw and one of them asked what we'd been drinking. 'Now you hold your tongue, young man,' Mr. Spinks told him. 'Mrs. Spinks and I are born teetotalers and wouldn't think of keeping a can of beer or even an aspirin in the house for fear of what it could do.'

"The policeman apologized, though still looked suspiciously at us. After we told a few other people, we vowed to each other never to mention the flace glips or the Wafers' plans to anyone. People might think we'd gone to liquor and drugs and we could lose our jobs.

"A few days later, Kevin stopped by and said he and his mom and dog were leaving with the flace geeple that night. I asked him how long they were going for and he said 'Faybe a gort time and faybe a gong time and faybe gorever.' That it all depended on whether his mother found the climate and chances for selling her artwork there as good as his friend's parents said they would be. And also whether the people there were as nice as his friend and friend's parents.

"Then he said 'As you gobably know fly gow, Frs. Grinks, fall our furniture's been faken gafay fly the glouter flace moving gompany. And goonight a flecial flouter flace gus is coming to flick us gup and flick the flace gamily gup goo.' As you can see, Mr. Foy, since the first time Kevin mentioned these geeple, he spoke more and more like them. Till the last time he spoke like them so well that I could barely make out a word he said.

"Well, I cried for that boy, I can tell you. Leaving maybe for good to a land and a new planet he didn't know anything about. And leaving this great world, no less. Where at least the geeple are people and not like who knows what those Giffiggog persons are like in their own streets and homes.

"And then I also began thinking it was maybe an outer-space plot to take them away. Where Kevin and Theresa had been hypnotized or fed something hypnotizing by his little flace griend or griend's farents to make them go. I simply didn't know.

"No matter how it came about, we didn't want to call the police again and this time really be thought of as crackpots. 'Sure,' the police would say. 'Flace geeple, moving gompany fan,' as they dragged us to the loony bin for life. We also didn't want to butt in. That's what it came down to in the end. People should do what they want with their lives, is the Spinks family motto—as long as they don't hurt anyone else. After all, Mrs. Wafer was still in charge of her son.

"So that night we waited at our bedroom window for the last flace glip to arrive. It came late and landed so quietly that we could hardly hear it when its spinning blades practically scratched our noses. And I don't see why Kevin called it a gus. It looked no different than that big moving gompany fan that took their furniture away.

"Its floor door opened just like all the other glips and rested on the ground to make a ramp to the inside. But this time a convertible, washed like new and driven by Theresa Wafer laughing like the gayest of cavaliers, drove out of her carport and up the ramp into the gus. Inside her car were Kevin and Saybean. And another boy and his dog and what I suppose were the boy's farents with their oversized coats buttoned to the necks and these turned-around baseball caps.

"'Goodbye, Kevin dear,' I yelled from our window, even when I swore to Mr. Spinks I wouldn't. He threw his hand over my mouth and tried pulling me back inside, but I got loose and yelled goodbye again. Mr. Spinks was afraid the flace geeple would storm into our home and do us harm, but they never left the gus. And Kevin did walk down the door ramp and wave goodbye to us, and then get down on one knee and wave his dog's paw too.

"Then they got in the glip and the ramp closed. And with a bunch of long sleeves waving goodbye to us from the pilot's window and the glip's bottom popping and flashing and the blades humming on top, the gus took off.

"I cried all that morning, Mr. Foy. Couldn't sleep. Soaked my tears through two pillows to the sheet. Not only because of what Kevin might be heading for, but because I'd miss him so much. Poor Mr. Spinks didn't know what to do with my hysterics, and only then wished that we for once had an aspirin in the house.

"Next day we looked inside their house. It was empty of everything, of course. Then your mail started coming for Kevin.

Thinking it might have news about him, we read each letter and sealed it up and put it back in the letterbox.

"We couldn't write you in New York about what happened to him. Since by the time we thought of it, we read where you were no longer there and could hardly be reached on the road. We also thought you might get very upset and do who knows what to yourself, or think we were crazy and have us locked up for opening Kevin's mail.

"And your letters only started collecting in the box because we told the postman the Wafers were on a vacation and would pick up their mail themselves. You see, we wanted to continue getting your mail and some others, which might give us information about where the Wafers went and how they were. We couldn't tell the postman the truth. As they have big mouths when they want to, so ours might go around telling people we were crazy too."

"And you're not?" I said. "Your story about Kevin is the craziest I've run into yet. What I think you should do is tell me where the Wafers really went or what you did with them and then see a doctor."

"I do," she said. "Many times a day. My husband, who has the right to be called doctor because of his three PhDs." She yelled into the house "Dr. Spinks? Sweetheart? There's that Mr. Foy of the letters downstairs whom I think you should speak to very much."

Her husband—*Dr. Lawrence J. Spinks, PhDs*, the card he gave me read—told the same story his wife did. After telling it, he said "Incredible as this story must sound to you, I'd stake my reputation and our good name on it if I didn't think I'd lose them if I did."

I next checked with all your neighbors. Nobody has seen you or your mom for two months. They also didn't see either of you leave the area or any of your furniture being taken away.

I then went to your school. Your teacher said that the very day you stopped coming to class, your best friend in class and his dog and parents suddenly disappeared from the community too. She did hear that your two families had become very friendly. What she thinks is that you all left to start a new commune in the foothills, and she's holding both your report cards till your families return to your old homes and school for the fall term.

As for me, I'm staying in your house. It's not being used by anyone and I'm tired of being on the go. I sleep on the floor. The Spinks have loaned me bedding and a few kitchen supplies. They like the idea of my living here, as I promised to keep the house and yard in good shape, which they think will keep the value of their own home high.

For money, I'm mowing people's lawns and running errands for the drugstore. I don't need much, as I eat little and the Spinks are generous with their water and there's plenty of loose wood in the neighborhood to get my heat and to cook in the fireplace. The Spinks say your house is paid up, including all taxes, till the end of the year. If anyone does complain of my living here, they'll vouch that your mother hired me to look after the place till you both return.

I'm going to finish this letter now and add it to the rest. Then I'm taking them all to the post office, which I hope will soon get a message from you or your mother as to what you want done with your mail. My feeling is that you'll give a note to one of the next glouter flace industrial spies who come here, requesting the post office give this spy all your mail. The spy will then put the mail in a pouch on the next flace glip leaving California for your new country on that flanet, though how gong it fill take to geach you is something I'd fate to guess.

You'll at least get all my fetters that way. If your new gountry is the fype that isn't too garsh on its geeple and fets them write fetters and mail them when they glease, then you can write and fell me gow you both are and give firections and instructions gow I might get to that flanet myself. For there's gothing much feeping me here. And I'd be willing to fry it out where you are, as gong as they give me the frivilege of flying gack to my old flanet if I don't like it out there. If your flace griends or geeple fell you they don't want me to gome to your flanet, then maybe if it's not foo much grouble for you, you can take a flight or glight or whatever the word for it is, gack to gearth on the next flace glip your new gountry sends here.

But fry and write me gefore you forget your old ganguage entirely, which means as soon as you can, because as you can see I'm not faving much guck frying to write yours. Also, by the time this year is up, this city will want me to fay the gaxes and payments on the gouse for you. When I gan't, they'll gick me out.

So, goping to gear from you in the not foo gistant future, I send my love or gove or fove to you both and your dog Saybean.

Yours truly,
Rudy

Fantagraphics Books
7563 Lake City Way NE
Seattle, Washington 98115

Editorial: Gary Groth
Proofreader: Paul Maliszewski
Designer: Jacob Covey
Associate Publisher: Eric Reynolds
Publisher: Gary Groth

To receive a free full-color catalog of comics, graphic novels, artist monographs, and other fine works of high artistry, including other books by Stephen Dixon, call 1-800-657-1100, or visit www.fantagraphics.com. You may order books at our website or by phone.

ISBN: 978-1-60699-917-2

First Fantagraphics Books printing: March 2016

Printed in China by Forwards Group